LUMINOUS AND FORLORN

Contemporary Short Stories by Women from Wales

Edited by

ELIN AP HYWEL

With a foreword by

JANE AARON

HONNO MODERN FICTION

Published by Honno
'Ailsa Craig', Heol y Cawl, Dinas Powys,
South Glamorgan, Wales, CF6 4AH.

First Impression 1994

© *The Authors 1994*

British Library Cataloguing in Publication Data

Luminous and Forlorn
1. Title

ISBN 1 870206 13 4

Published with the financial support of the
Arts Council of Wales

Acknowledgements

The following stories in this collection have been published
or broadcast elsewhere:

'Charity' by Clare Morgan first appeared in *Planet* (1994);
'Luminous and Forlorn' by Siân James was broadcast on Radio 4
in September 1992; 'Helsinki Mouse' by Penny Windsor appeared
in *Cambrensis* (8) in Autumn 1989, and 'Red Roses for a Blue Lady'
by Christine Harrison was broadcast on Radio 4 in March 1993.

Cover illustration by Emma Taylor

Cover design by Ruth Dineen

Typeset and printed in Wales by Gwasg Dinefwr, Llandybïe

CONTENTS

Biographical Notes	vi
Foreword by Jane Aaron	ix
Luminous and Forlorn – Siân James	1
Solo Conversation – Kusha Petts	12
The Glass Porch – Patricia Duncker	19
Red Roses for a Blue Lady – Christine Harrison	27
Mustard – Catherine Merriman	37
A Step Away from Trouble – Catherine Merriman	41
A Place in Wales – Clare Morgan	53
Punishment – Tessa Hadley	66
Killing the Hay – Julie Raynsbury	74
Helsinki Mouse – Penny Windsor	83
The Win – Alexandra Ward	90
A Very Private Affair – Christine Harrison	96
Clouded Gem – Kusha Petts	104
My Sarah – Julie Raynsbury	112
Poor Players – Rhian Thomas	128
Lovey-Dovey Cats' Eyes – Jacqueline Jacques	135
Charity – Clare Morgan	140
Two Children – Danw November	151
Sonata – Alexandra Ward	166
Mary Kate – Jenny Sullivan	172
Hester and Louise – Siân James	178

BIOGRAPHICAL NOTES

PATRICIA DUNCKER was born in Jamaica and has been travelling ever since. She now teaches in the English Department at the University of Wales, Aberystwyth. She has published short fiction and articles in numerous academic and literary reviews and is the author of *Sisters and Strangers: an Introduction to Contemporary Feminist Fiction* (Blackwell, 1992). She lives in France for part of the year and finds the enormous differences between France and Wales traumatic and interesting.

TESSA HADLEY was born in Bristol in 1956 and read English at Cambridge. She is joint author of two collections of stories for children and has written a monologue for radio which was broadcast on Radio Wales. She is completing an MA in Creative Writing at Bath College of Higher Education and is about to embark on a Ph.D. on Henry James. At present she is working on a novel. She is married with three children and has lived in Cardiff for the last twelve years.

CHRISTINE HARRISON was born on the Isle of Wight in 1933. She lived in many different places before settling near Fishguard some eighteen years ago. She began writing short stories a few years ago, and has won numerous prizes, including the Cosmopolitan Short Story Award. In 1991 she was the recipient of a writer's bursary from the Welsh Arts Council. Her novel *Airy Cages* was published by Macmillan in March. She has been married twice and has three daughters and nine grandchildren.

JACQUELINE JACQUES was born in Tŷ Croes on Anglesey. She now lives in Essex, where she works as a special needs teacher. She is married and has two children.

SIÂN JAMES was born in south Cardiganshire. She later moved to live in Aberystwyth and was educated at Ardwyn Grammar School and the University College of Wales, Aberystwyth. For thirty years she was married to the Shakespearian actor, Emrys James, who died in 1989, and she has four grown-up children. Her six published novels to date include *A Small Country* (Collins, 1979) which was reissued by Seren in 1989. A seventh novel, *A Storm in Arberth* (Seren) is due to appear this year. She has twice won the Yorkshire Post Prize for fiction.

CATHERINE MERRIMAN was born in London in 1949 and has lived near Brynmawr in Gwent since 1973. She has worked as a statistician, a playgroup organiser, a barmaid, an adult education officer and an officer for an environmental organisation, as well as being a volunteer worker for Abergavenny Women's Aid for eleven years. She is the author of a collection of short stories, *Silly Mothers* (Honno, 1991) and two novels, *Leaving the Light On* (Gollancz, 1992; Pan Macmillan, 1994) and *Fatal Observations* (Gollancz, 1993).

CLARE MORGAN was born just outside Monmouth. She has published one novel, *A Touch of the Other* (Gollancz) and many short stories, some of which have appeared in *The New Penguin Book of Welsh Short Stories* (1993) and the British Council anthology *New Writing*. She now divides her time between Dinas Mawddwy and Oxford.

KUSHA PETTS was born in London; one of her grandmothers was Welsh. After taking a degree in Fine Arts, specialising in painting, she taught for a time. Between 1947 and 1983 she was married to John Petts, the artist and craftsman, and for many years was his workshop assistant in stained glass and mosaic. She has published one collection of poetry, *Necklace for a Poor Sod* (Gomer), and her work has been included in a number of anthologies, including *Parachutes and Petticoats* (Honno, 1993), and used on Radio 4 and BBC 2. She lives at Llansteffan in Dyfed. Over the past ten years she has resumed painting and showing her work in exhibitions.

JULIE RAYNSBURY was born in Kent and studied English Literature at the University of Newcastle-upon-Tyne. She has lived and worked in west Wales since 1978. Her first novel for children, *The Seventh Seal*, was published by Gomer in 1993 and her poems have appeared in a number of magazines. She is a student on the new MA course in Creative Writing at the University of Glamorgan.

JENNY SULLIVAN was born in Cardiff, but has lived in Raglan in Gwent since 1980. She has written professionally for many years, and became a full-time writer/tutor in January 1994. She is a member of the Arts Council of Wales' Writers on Tour scheme and enjoys encouraging the craft of writing in anyone who is interested, especially children. Her children's novel *The Magic Apostrophe* will be published by Pont Books this year and she has just completed a sequel.

RHIAN THOMAS hails from Anglesey, and most of her writing is inspired by the island itself. She is presently studing for a degree in Russian and French at Nottingham University.

ALEXANDRA WARD hails from south Wales and now lives in Llanfihangel-y-Creuddyn in Ceredigion. As a child she attended too many schools to recount in detail, but her serious education began in the late sixties when she became a student at Coleg Harlech. From there she went on to University College, Cardiff to read English and later did research at the University of East Anglia. As well as numerous short stories, she has written two unpublished (and destroyed) romantic novels and is now working on a third novel. She is married and has one daughter.

PENNY WINDSOR was born in 1946. Although Cornish, she has lived and worked in Swansea for many years, where she is now a full-time writer and performance poet. She has published three volumes of poetry: *Dangerous Women* and *Like Oranges* (both from Honno) and *Crashing the Moon* (Pen-y-Craig Community Press). She has had short stories published in many magazines, including *Stand*, *Planet*, and *Cambrensis*. She is also a traveller and the mother of two daughters.

FOREWORD

•

Jane Aaron

'Luminous and Forlorn', the tale which gives its title to this collection of short stories by women living in Wales, captures the quick-changing moods of a teenage girl during one evening in a Welsh seaside town some thirty or forty years ago. Her lust for life is chequered by the pressure of parental expectations and by the perpetual background beat of the sea. Walking home from a party with an unexpected partner, the narrator of Siân James's story notices how 'our shadows go before us' along the moonlit street. As an image of present consciousness stepping on towards a future shaped by the shadowy hand of the past, her phrase is evocative of the drift of many of the stories gathered together in this volume.

Frequently, the chief protagonist in the tales is an older woman who, looking back at her life, sees its early promise as circumscribed. In Kusha Petts's 'Clouded Gem', for example, the ageing wife of a fish and chip shop proprietor, struggling to maintain the business with little help from her indolent husband, remembers how during her youthful period of infatuation with the same man she noticed with pity the rough mating of a pair of cats who could hardly be credited with an ecstasy of feeling equivalent to her own. But now she thinks: 'life's like that. Life's like an old tom cat that gets you by the scruff of the neck and you can't get free.' And in Clare Morgan's 'Charity', Marged, who featured in her youth as Mad Marge the all-in wrestler, experiences herself in middle age as 'getting smaller and smaller' every day, hemmed in more than she ever was in the ring by a life 'made up of back yards, and half-turned earth. And the walls of the houses going up very straight, and the roofs, in layers, angling back over themselves.'

In terms of both theme and style, stories such as these are reminiscent of short fictions composed much earlier in this century by women in Wales. In 'Mrs Pike's Eldorado', a tale from Margiad Evans's fine collection *The Old and the Young* (1948), Mrs Pike, having found sanctuary with her sister Maria from the wreck of a second disastrous marriage, pronounces judgement on her life:

> She lifted her arm in a dull gesture and then she uttered what was possibly the only passionate reference to her life she ever made. 'It's terrible. It's terrible. I was a-looking at the sun rising in the train. Maria! don't tha feel … it be just as if summat was stolen from you every d'y? We don't never get the day as we do see rising. No never. We do see it over there with the sun rising and then summat else do seem to slip in, like, and that un be what we do get.'

Similarly, in Hilda Vaughan's beautifully wrought story 'A Thing of Nought' (1934), Megan Lloyd, after the loss of the 'child of my dreams' who bore an extraordinary resemblance to the object of her unconsummated desire, experiences herself as kin to the shadows passing to and fro across her valley all day long, leaving no trace of their passage behind. And in the stories of Dorothy Edwards, who threw herself under a train at the age of thirty-one, the same sense prevails of stunted lives half-lived, of characters shunted to the side of their own experiences, with something – passion, meaning, a sense of reality – stolen from them every day.

And yet it cannot be said that the similarities of mood which exist between some of the stories in this present collection and the texts from the past are indications of an established tradition of Welsh women's English-language shorter fiction. For no such tradition has ever been recognised: women's short stories have been shunted into the margins of the canon of Welsh writing in English as inexorably as their protagonists have characteristically found themselves relegated to marginal existences. It is not so much that the women's texts have not been republished and do not feature on the English-language syllabuses of schools and higher education institutions, for that same fate continues to beset their story-writing brothers, and yet there does exist a strongly established tradition of English-language shorter fiction by Welsh men. Nor is it so much that the women's contribution has been entirely ignored by anthologists of the Welsh short story. So far, at least nine anthologies purporting to represent the best of twentieth-century Welsh short stories have been published. On average, about 17 per cent, or one in six, of the writers included in these collections have been women, a fraction which compares favourably enough with the usual allocation of space to women writers in literary anthologies, which is generally closer to the one in twelve mark.

What renders a female tradition invisible, however, is the anthologists' lack of consistency when it comes to the decision as to which female writers to include. The representation of male authors in these volumes is remarkably consistent. When the first collection of Welsh short stories was published by Faber in 1937 it included a phalanx of names which have regularly reappeared in every subsequent anthology – Caradoc Evans, Rhys Davies, Geraint Goodwin, Glyn Jones, Gwyn Jones, and Dylan Thomas. In

the next anthology, published in 1940, Alun Lewis featured
for the first time; in 1956 Gwyn Thomas made his début; in
1959 Emyr Humphreys was added; in 1970 Leslie Norris; in
1976 Ron Berry and Alun Richards; and in 1988 Dannie
Abse and Duncan Bush. Not one of these authors, after his
initial inclusion, was omitted from the team of 'classic' Welsh
story-writers. By contrast, the names of women bob up and
down like corks on the contents sheets. In 1937, Hilda
Vaughan, Dorothy Edwards and Margiad Evans were all
included in the Faber collection (along with five other female
authors – women were never subsequently to have it so
good). In 1940, in Gwyn Jones's first anthology, all three
were dropped, and Hilda Vaughan's name was never in
fact to feature in the lists again. In 1956 Margiad Evans
reappeared, but Dorothy Edwards was still missing, whereas
in 1959 Dorothy Edwards made a come-back but now
Margiad Evans was absent. The 1970 anthology, edited by
Sam Adams and Roland Mathias, solved the problem by
ignoring the women altogether, and opting for an all-male
line-up. But in 1971 Margiad Evans was back, though
Dorothy Edwards was not omitted. Both were absent from
Alun Richards's Penguin anthology of 1976 but Brenda
Chamberlain was now included for the first time. She was
still in the team in 1988, in John Davies's anthology, which
also found space for both Margiad Evans and Dorothy
Edwards. All three writers were missing from Alun Richards's
second collection of 1993, however, though this volume did
include Glenda Beagan and Clare Morgan who had both
made their first appearance in the anthologies in 1988. As
far as individual female story-writers are concerned, then,
it seems to be generally a case of 'now you see them, now
you don't'; consequently not one of them can be said to
have gained recognition as an indispensable contributor to

the genre, and no foundations have been laid for the development of a specifically female tradition in Welsh story-
writing in English.

In fact, many anthologists have made a particular point
of stressing the 'macho' qualities of the Welsh short story in
English, and consequently of debarring the weaker sex
from any vital role in the game. The genre is generally inter-
preted as having been created in Wales as part of a protest-
ing masculine response to the social crisis of the industrial
south during the 1920s and 1930s, with its devastating effects
on male employment. Male sporting imagery is rife throughout the anthologies' introductory pages. Gwyn Jones's
account of the differences between the Welsh and the Anglo-
Welsh short story is particularly revealing in gender terms.
The stories of the Welsh-language writers Kate Roberts and
Eigra Lewis Roberts belong he says, quoting H. E. Bates on
Kate Roberts, to 'the literature of still waters'. The work of
their male colleagues, D. J. Williams and John Gwilym Jones,
'are the masculine counterparts of these feminine achieve-
ments, richer-textured, warmer hued, with a fuller rhythm,
and more joyfully redolent of soil, people, feast and cere-
monies.' Yet they still share with the women qualities of
'composure and decorum' ... 'to an extent neither inherent
in, nor much sought by, the Anglo-Welsh, who so frequently
reach for a heightened subject matter, a highly-wrought
diction, and a high-powered narrative convention' (Jones,
1971). If women, by virtue of their gender-specific inhibitions,
cannot achieve the fuller if still decorous tones of the Welsh-
language male writers, what chance have they of emulating
the revved-up roaring of the Anglo-Welsh? No wonder that
the female Welsh writer in English has no place in this com-
parison.

What, one wonders, would Gwyn Jones have made of

some of the stories included in Honno's present collection? 'Composure and decorum' are not qualities which, on the face of it, seem integral to such shattering tales as Patricia Duncker's 'The Glass Porch', or Jacqueline Jacques's gothic 'Lovey-Dovey Cats' Eyes', and revving it up is of the essence in Catherine Merriman's biker story. Actually, I can guess what he would have said: he would probably have protested, 'But half these writers are not Welsh! They are not of the blood of our stoic sisters.' Honno's policy of embracing all women who live in Wales, regardless of their place of birth, as within their catchment area for new writing would have provided the Achilles heel with which to dismiss this collection as unrepresentative of the muted inglorious Mams of Wales. But the anthology was never intended as a mirror of 'true' Welsh womanhood; rather, it represents, simply and straightforwardly, the editor's choice from amongst some of the liveliest writings recently submitted to Honno Press.

As such, however, it does break through historical barriers: its very existence, as the first anthology of short stories from Wales with an all-female line-up, is enough in itself to make us question the old shibboleths. And for all that some of the stories on the following pages do movingly echo the painful and enforced resignation characteristic of many of the earlier texts published by women in Wales – a resignation which, in its convincing exposure of disappointment and the wastage of female potential on a massive scale, constitutes in itself a form of protest; others do break free of that mould, and in so doing are not entirely unrepresentative of women's lives in contemporary Wales. Although the main purpose of this collection is to entertain rather than inform, with the publication of this volume, the Honno co-operative can, at the very least, be said to have taken another step towards its goal of redressing the unequal gender balance and the sexual stereotyping within Welsh literary traditions.

LUMINOUS AND FORLORN

•

Siân James

'You can come to my place tonight,' Neville whispers to me before school on Monday. 'My parents are having a night out. What do you say? We can have some wine and some beans on toast and we'll dance after. What do you say?'

'Oh Neville, I don't know. I've got my Milton essay to finish and you know I'm only allowed out on Saturday.'

His eyes hold mine. 'Make some excuse. Say there's something on. Something educational. Come on. We'll have a great time.'

He squeezes my hand before I rush off to my prefect duties. Neville is incredibly handsome. He looks like a young Cary Grant. Everyone says so. Eyes brown as toffee and the same cleft in the chin. All the same, I know I won't be able to persuade my mother to let me go out with him on a Monday.

She's never met Neville, but even so, she's dead set against him, her lips becoming thin as little whips whenever I mention his name.

His family is English, which is bad enough, and they keep a licensed restaurant – which is worse. 'Pubs are one thing,' my mother says. 'Pubs are the known enemy. But when cafés, which have always been decent places where decent people can go, start to offer alcoholic drinks, well, it's the thin end of the wedge and a trap to the unwary.'

The way my mother brings out 'alcoholic drinks' you

know it's no use trying to break it to her that Neville is your boyfriend.

She doesn't object to you having 'friends of the opposite sex', but she won't have anything serious that might put you off your studies, mind. And in any case, she wouldn't have Neville. What she'd really like is if I still went out to the pictures with Nia Gruffydd every Saturday night, because Nia Gruffydd is one of those girls who wear pleated skirts and hair bands and no trace of make-up. Oh, she's nice enough, but I often wonder if she isn't a bit retarded. She's the same age as me, going on seventeen, but she looks fourteen, with a chest instead of a woman's body, and her idea of a good time is to go to hear Côr-y-Castell rehearsing.

Anyway, my mother idolizes her, because her mother writes articles in the *Cymro* and gives talks on the wireless.

'If you pass your exams and go to University, you can become a WEA lecturer like Nia Gruffydd's mother,' she's always saying.

Nia's got a brother called Garmon and I'm sure my mother's secret dream is that he'll fall for me one day. She's always asking after him. He's in his second year at Bangor doing Welsh and Philosophy or something, and of course a safe, long-distance courtship by letter would suit her down to the ground.

'Garmon's going back at the weekend,' Nia tells me in History, which is our first lesson. It's funny, but she's really fond of her brother, though he's so fat and sweaty. Once I called for her and the sitting-room ponged of feet, which must have been him, because whatever you can say about Nia, her personal habits are exemplary.

'Would you and Garmon like to come to a party tonight?' I ask her.

'A party?'

Her big round eyes seem about to pop out of her head. For a moment I imagine two lumps of blue jelly landing on her history textbook.

'A party,' I say, trying to sound cool. 'At Neville's. His parents are going out. We can have sandwiches and wine. And we can dance.'

'I can only do the quickstep,' Nia says. 'Don't ask me to rock-around-the-clock, will you.'

We both smile. Sometimes I think the girl's got the beginnings of a sense of humour.

Miss Mathias comes in then and just before we settle down to the Repeal of the Corn Act 1842, I feel a cold shiver at my cunning. I've managed it. Got my way again. My mother would never refuse to let me go to a party with Nia and Garmon Gruffydd.

Neville doesn't seem to mind that I've asked Nia and her brother to join us. 'More the merrier,' he says. 'Brynmor's coming along as well. To play the piano.'

I toss my hair back – it's something I've been practising in the mirror. 'Brynmor's always following us around. He's got a piano at home.'

'I know. But his mother doesn't like him playing dance music.'

Poor dab. Brynmor's mother is worse than mine. Not only chapel three times every Sunday, but prayer meeting and Band of Hope as well.

All the same, I wish he didn't have to follow us about everywhere, it's inhibiting for one thing, and humiliating too.

Neville and I park ourselves in one of the little shelters on the prom for a snog, and bloody Brynmor turns up and stands about in front of us and starts talking about Yeats or Schubert or someone, as though that's what we're there for. I suppose it's worse for Nev than for me because he doesn't have the slightest interest in poetry or music. God, I never mind having a natter with Brynmor at the right time and place, but when you're sprawled out over somebody, hoping for some sort of vibrant sensual experience, it's just not on.

'Brynmor, go away, will you?'

And what I really can't take is that it's usually me, not Neville, begging him to take the long walk on the short pier.

When you come to think of it, Neville is pretty half-hearted as a lover. His kisses, for instance, are so long and gentle that I could honestly plan out my homework while they're going on and sometimes do. On and on, never changing gear, never reaching any next step.

He never even tries to stroke my breasts, doesn't even try to locate them.

Perhaps I'm lacking in something. Everyone whistles at me, but when I'm in a clinch with someone, they don't half get apathetic.

Islwyn Ellis, this boy I went out with before Neville, at least he used to get a bit excited when he started fiddling with the buttons of my blouse. Only when he'd managed to get them undone, he always started grunting, and in the dark, I used to imagine he'd turned into a little pig and used to push him away. At least Neville is handsome and six foot tall and at least he doesn't grunt.

My mother is one of these people who's always full of jolly little precepts like, 'It's up to a girl to say no.'

My God, chance would be a fine thing.

'How would you feel on your wedding night,' my mother asks me, 'if you'd already given away your greatest treasure?'

My God, no one's ever made any serious bid for my greatest treasure. It'll be really great having to admit that on my wedding night.

Neville rings me every single evening, hangs about me every lunchtime, writes me long, boring letters with terrible spelling when he thinks I'm in a bad mood, but as for his love-making, it's nothing short of pathetic. Do I really want to go on going out with him? Sometimes his five-minute kisses make me feel I could be doing something else. Like running a mile for instance.

Why do people force you into telling lies? I feel really depressed at having to give my mother all that stuff about Nia and Garmon. 'Garmon is very keen that I go with them. He's going back to college next week.' I can imagine her planning her announcement to Mrs Williams next door. 'Yes, she's got engaged, Mrs Williams fach. To Garmon Gruffydd. Yes. Delia Gruffydd's son. Her that's on the wireless every Sunday night in 'Wedi'r Oedfa'. Yes, her only son. Oh yes, Mrs Williams, Welsh to the fingertips. No, Baptist actually, but as long as it's chapel, Morris and I don't mind.'

Why do people make it so difficult for other people, when all they want is to be truthful and decent.

I take ages getting ready. It's not that I want to look particularly terrific or anything like that. It's just that everything is suddenly a bit of a drag. I've made some notes for my *Lycidas* essay and I wouldn't really mind staying in and being able to get to grips with it.

I hope to God I'm not going to turn into one of these intellectual types. Someone in a Welsh tapestry two-piece who's into *cyd-adrodd*. Anyway, I don't look like one. Not yet. As a matter of fact I look more like a photographic model tonight, my breasts pulled up high in front of me in my new Loveable bra. I could be in the running for Miss Cambrian Coast next year, only of course my mother wouldn't hear of me going in for it. So common.

'Yes Mam, I'll be back by eleven. Don't worry, will you. Yes, I'll be all right.'

Of course I bloody will. Same as ever.

I dawdle along the prom.

It's September and the town is ours again; the two chip shops and the milk bar almost empty.

The tide is out and the seaweed smells green and rich. Usually I only like staring out to sea when I've got an ice-cream to lick; the cold sweet taste of ice-cream goes really well with the tangy smell of the sea. (I love smelling, and eating; all the vulgar pleasures.)

Tonight the sea is calm, its colour almost all drained away. Whitish sky and pale grey sea. But with light in it. Luminous is a brilliant word. I often use it in essays.

I nearly drowned by those rocks when I was about thirteen.

I was allowed to swim from the first of May, and that year, even though the weather turned cold and stormy, I couldn't make myself wait any longer.

No one else was stupid enough to join me.

God, I must have been mad. After only a few seconds I knew I was in danger. The waves were so high that I couldn't go on swimming. The sea kept sucking me up and throwing me down again and after four or five times, I remember the realisation seeping through me that there was absolutely nothing for it but to give up.

But the very next wave threw me against those rocks and I was able to scramble to my feet and stand there, gulping and gasping like a fish in a bucket.

Even wading back was difficult. It was as though the sea was having second thoughts about letting me go.

When I got to the beach, there was a man standing there; in a brown tweed overcoat, I remember. 'You bloody fool,' he said. That's all. 'You bloody fool.'

I pulled my towel round me and was sick, almost at his feet. I remember the sand steaming as I covered it up.

I remember my cotton vest scratching like emery paper as I pulled it on.

Even my face was bruised by the pebbles the sea had flung at me.

I told my mother I'd had a fall.

Tonight, there's only the faintest breeze ruffling the luminous water.

'The Bay Restaurant. Licensed to sell alcoholic beverages.' Neville's house is the last on the prom; tall and grey with flashy red paint. A notice in the window. Closed.

Even from across the road I can hear Brynmor Roberts playing away. That old one, 'Begin the Beguine'. For a moment I stand listening. It sounds restless and forlorn with the seagulls mewing in the background. Forlorn is another of my favourite words.

Brynmor is a bit of a joke at school because he composes oratorios which we have to sing in Assembly. But he can certainly play Cole Porter. He can play proper music too for that matter, Beethoven and that lot. He improvises a little fanfare when I go in.

Garmon Gruffydd is sitting at one of the tables with a half-full bottle of red wine in front of him. 'Come to join me,' he says, his voice full and fruity like Mr Isaacs, the minister.

They've got a bit of a dance floor in the middle of the room, and what do you know, Neville is there cheek-to-cheek with my little pal Nia Gruffydd. And gosh, Nia is looking almost pretty. She's washed her long straight hair and it's yellow as Madeira cake and she's wearing it in a loose pageboy instead of tied back like a kid. She's got a pale blue angora wool sweater on, and, so help me, she's even got little pointy breasts under there.

I'm usually in a tearing fury if any girl so much as glances at Neville, but tonight I feel tolerant, even good-humoured. The thing is, they look really happy together. He seems much more relaxed with her than he does with me and she's gazing up at him as though she's Cinderella and it's two minutes to twelve. When the music stops, they start walking over towards me but I raise my glass and smile at them and Brynmor launches into something else and they go on dancing and staring at each other.

I take a swig of the wine Garmon's poured out for me. It doesn't seem all it's cracked up to be in poetry; that wine and roses stuff. In fact it tastes a bit like Gee's Linctus. I suppose it's about as romantic as cocoa if you think of it as alcoholic beverage. I drink about half a glassful and then Garmon asks me to dance.

I get to my feet, neither eager nor reluctant. Garmon is certainly not the most desirable partner in the world, but what choice have I got?

He dances quite well, but I wish I didn't keep thinking abut his podgy little hands on my back. He does some fancy turns and breathes down my neck. How much of the alcoholic beverage has he drunk, I wonder? And his mother the champion of total abstinence. I feel quite sorry for Mrs Gruffydd, her son on the red stuff and her daughter in the arms of Neville Cooper of no fixed religion, whose one ambition in life is to get his O-level Maths so that he can join the Marines.

It becomes clear that I'm going to have to dance with Garmon all evening. Well, it would be unfair to expect Nia to dance with her brother I suppose. Especially when she's looking so many fathoms deep in love with my bloody Neville. But does ghastly Garmon have to press me so tight? Yes, I know about holding your partner close, but this is suffocation. And when I draw in a deep breath, expanding my chest, the nasty little slug gets the idea I'm being provocative.

'I bet you're hot stuff,' he says, nibbling my ear.

'And I bet you're never going to find out,' I say, breaking away from him and pushing him backwards into a chair.

'I'm going home,' I tell Brynmor.

'I'll get Nev.'

I look over at where he and Nia are sitting close together, drinking lemonade.

'No, leave him be. He's happy.'

'I'll come with you then.'

'OK. Neville won't notice.'

We let ourselves out into the silent town. 'I didn't know you were nice as well,' Brynmor says.

Why should I bother to flirt with Brynmor. 'As well as what?' Why should I say it? I know that I'm competently put together and prettily coloured-in too; brown hair, brown freckles, blue eyes, pink nipples.

When we get to the pier, we stand listening to the sea

dribbling onto the pebbles. 'Do you know the Sea Symphony?' he asks me, 'By Vaughan Williams?' His head moves in time to some forlorn music.

' "For Lycidas is dead",' I say, ' "dead ere his prime".' Tears sting my eyes. I want to live for ever.

'Debussy,' Brynmor says, 'Franz Mahler, César Franck.' He sounds like someone praying.

' "Who would not sing for Lycidas? He knew himself to sing and build the lofty rhyme. He must not float upon his watery bier unwept and … something in the parching winds".'

'Welter,' Brynmor says.

'Yes. "He must not float upon his watery bier unwept and welter in the parching winds".'

'I might set that to music,' Brynmor says. 'Cello and a lot of percussion. Milton's *Lycidas* in E minor.'

'I nearly got drowned once,' I tell him. 'Out by those rocks … of course I shouldn't have gone in. It was very stormy.'

A moment's silence. 'Anyone can make a mistake,' he says then.

We turn towards the town. Terrace Road. Bath Street. Past the chapel where he plays the organ. He tells me I can come to listen to him practising. Anytime.

Our shadows go before us. Brynmor used to be a midget, but now he's nearly as tall as I am. Curly-haired and eagle nosed. 'It was a good party,' he says after a while, 'but I don't think I'm going to come all the way up Penglais with you.'

'That's OK,' I say. 'It's no distance from here.'

For a minute or two we lean against the wall of a house

in Maesderw Road and watch the moon come out from behind a cloud and the sky lighten. 'Farewell, sweet prince,' I say then, and start to run up the hill. I can still hear sea music in my head, and I'm alive, alive.

SOLO CONVERSATION
•
Kusha Petts

Right. So. He hasn't come. Oh well, that's that. So he hasn't come. He's … anywhere. Nowhere. I'm nowhere.

What did you expect?

Well, obviously too much. He said he'd be here and I must have expected him to be here.

Jesus Christ! Why did you expect?

Yes, why ever did I expect him to mean what he said? Why should anyone mean anything?

Haven't you learnt anything at all?

Oh, why must I feel so damn sick? This lousy constriction of the throat …

Can't you be sensible? Commonsensical?

God, there ought to be a nice handy dose to buy at – say – Boots or some corner chemist. 'Please, I want a bottle of anti-let-down-at-seven-on-Friday mixture.' Analgesic bliss. Or some fantastic emulsion to make you feel all beautiful inside, as if you knew you loved someone and they knew you knew. And they loved you too. If only for a little while.

Oh, wouldn't that sell well. Go like a bomb.

You're going to cry.

No I'm not.

You are, you know. You'll make that awful face in the mirror. Pour yourself a little drinkie, dear, instead.

No, I won't. Daddie always did that. Probably still doing

it somewhere. Wherever that is. And with whoever he hopes is now his bundle of joy.

Why aren't you used to this feeling? You should be, you know. It's only variations on a theme. Flat champagne. Empty Easter eggs. Fizzled fireworks. Etcetera. Remember the first time? How old were you? Seven?

Seven ... eight ... something like that. Who cares?

There I was, nearly ill with excitement in the beginning, waiting at Heathrow for the plane. Going to Cannes for six whole weeks, six summer weeks I lived for all the year.

Ingrid was au pair then. She was nice. You were sorry when she went. But after a year she said she was homesick for Sweden.

Maybe she'd had enough of our house, too.

What a pest you were on journeys. Every year you insisted on going on the midday plane because you loved pushing the tray-rest up and down and being served lunch. You wasted most of it, asked for squash you didn't drink, went to the loo for no good reason, took your cardigan on and off. Hell, why didn't someone sit on you?

It was the first time Ingrid had taken me on a plane and she couldn't understand how to fill in the landing form so she asked the woman in the window seat.

Then the woman asked you your name.

'Valerie Edwige. The Edwige is French because of my mummie's daddie's mummie. And she's very old but she's still alive.'

She said would you like to change places so that you could look down on the bobbly cotton-wool clouds and watch out for the Alps. Then you told her all about the Pichard family and how you went out there every year and how they'd all be waiting at the airport at Nice and – most important of all – you told her about Pierre and how you loved him and how he'd do anything you asked.

'Pierre will be waiting for me to come,' I told her. 'He's really Ta-ta Jeannine's family but she lets him sleep in my room and I love that.'

Of course you did. Your own room in Avebury Square was very pretty and full of lovely toys, but there was no one to share. And dolls don't breathe however much you pretend.

The woman helped you cut up your chicken and sliced those giant strawberries they always serve. She seemed to understand how important Pierre was. She said she'd thought Ingrid was your mother when you boarded the plane.

'Oh no. Mummie isn't coming. She's already gone to Paris. Well, *near* Paris. To ride. And Daddie's going to Germany. It's just me, with Ingrid. And we'll stay *all* summer and Pierre will come everywhere with us and join in *everything*.'

You had your favourite dress on. Lavender. Mummie always said it was nice with your hair. Your hair was about all she praised. But she did her best for you. Clothes and so on.

I wasn't exactly promising material for her, was I? Not quite the child she should have produced.

And though you liked to look at horses you were scared of them, while Mummie just adored them and could do anything with them.

Oh, Mummie and Daddie were quite sweet to you in their separate ways …

Always: 'Yes, darling. Of course darling. A birthday party. Just tell Berthe who you'd like to come, and to phone Forte's.'

And, 'No, darling. Daddie can't be here. He's simply absolutely got to be in Venice.'

Or somewhere.

Or, 'No, darling, you'll be staying with Daddie. And Berthe, of course.' There was always a Berthe or a Helga or an Ingrid.

You'd been allowed to stay up to dine with them the night before Mummie was due to fly to Paris. You thought she was going to the Meuniers', where she always rode, and, thinking to please her with her favourite topic, you kept asking her about the horses and were there any new ones and what were their names. Names were so important; animals' as much as people's.

And she wasn't answering me directly so I said: 'You *are* going to ride, aren't you, Mummie?'

It was after dinner and she'd curled up in a low chair. Daddie was by the hearth, though there wasn't any fire, of course, and he was sipping his brandy. He looked at her over the top of his glass and said in a funny sort of voice: 'Oh yes. Mummie's bound to be going to … *ride*. Aren't you, Louise, my sweet?' And Mummie said nothing. Absolutely nothing. She just uncurled her legs – she had a short dress on and I'd been disappointed; I'd wanted her to wear one of her lovely long dresses as it was a special evening for me – but she just uncurled her beautiful legs and stretched them out in front of her, crossed one ankle over the other and lay back staring up at Daddie with her eyes half-closed. And she ran her hands through her hair, spreading it out like dark wings each side of her head.

Then Daddie said something to her very rapidly in French and you couldn't understand. All you caught was – sûr et certain – à cheval – and you thought it was about horses! But she didn't answer. Only opened her blue eyes very wide at him and pursed her lips as if she'd kiss him. He turned his back on her then and went to pour himself more brandy.

And I didn't know what was going on. Really! Children are pathetic. Bamboozled.

Coming in to land at Nice, I did remember to thank the woman who'd given me her seat, but I couldn't get off fast enough. I felt like pushing everyone in front of me. Over the barrier I caught a glimpse of the heads of the dear Pichard family and at last there they were, hugging and kissing me and saying how I'd grown. Then I was looking about for Pierre.

But he wasn't anywhere. And they looked so solemn when I asked where he was. They said: 'He couldn't come.' Oh, they must be playing a silly game, I thought. Hadn't I once heard grand'tante Laure say – when she'd overheard the maid Victorine laughing with grandpère in his study – 'Oh, Louis. Le bon blageur.' I'd asked her what she meant and she said grandpère was a sort of joker. And she ruffled my hair and held my face in her hands and said she supposed we were all jokers one way or another, which I didn't understand. There were lots of people I knew who couldn't possibly be jokers. Still, grandpère did love a tease. So he must be teasing now. It must be some sort of joke. Pierre must be in the car. Or just left at home.

But he wasn't. Pierre was dead. They broke it as gently as they could. It had happened the day before. He'd slipped his lead and run after a ball some wretched holiday boy had bounced into the road. And it was all terribly unfortunate but a car had hit him. He was too hurt to be made well, and he was getting old and did I realize he couldn't have lived much longer, anyway. Little dogs can't live very long. The vet had put him gently to sleep. And they were terribly, terribly sad too, truly they were, and they knew just how I felt but I mustn't cry so, I really mustn't.

Oh mustn't I. What did the sun matter now? Or the sea? Or the palm trees that I always said looked as if they were growing out of pineapples? Where was Pierre with his bony little body under that so-silky fur, his bright eyes and his wet nose that he pushed into my hand? And the way he had of suddenly sitting still with just the tip of his tongue peeping out. So stupid and so funny. I used to sing him a silly verse I'd made up. Kids' stuff:

> Mon petit petit petit
> petit Pierre
> je suis je suis je suis
> ta grande amie
> et ta petite mère.

I loved him. He loved me. Every year he loved me. It was unbearable that he simply *wasn't* any more. What was being dead, anyway? I couldn't believe he'd never make me squeal and hop, licking my bare toes when I got out of bed each morning. He wasn't there – yet I kept feeling my fingers running through his fur. He wasn't there – but I kept expecting him to come dashing around the corner.

How can you break your heart over a ridiculous little apricot poodle? But I did. I really did. I cried so much my head ached, my face was all puffy and my chest hurt. At night I got so feverish that bonne-maman kept coming into my room, stroking my hair. She was sweet but it didn't help. Promised a kitten I didn't want. Said we could drive up to Grasse to see cousine Simone. Me – I didn't care if I never saw Simone again. I only wanted what I couldn't have – Pierre.

Little Pierre. What fun we'd had. And I'd never once thought it would end ... Oh, you were good for me, little Pierre, dying when you did. You were my first real lesson. *Nota bene*: one must never indulge in expectation.

Yet I have been.

Black mark, Val, old girl.

Huh! Do you remember fat Miss Brandon with your prep?
'You tiresome child, Valerie Barrington, am I never to expect

better work from you?' (Yes, ma'am, no ma'am, three bags full ma'am.) And a black mark. Or that good old-fashioned punishment, a hundred lines.

Better take some now.

Write – and do not tie two pens together and try to cheat – write: I must not indulge in expectation. A hundred times. Two hundred times. No. A thousand times.

Oh, no, no, no. Just write: 'I must remember Pierre.'

You do, you do remember Pierre.

Maybe I will have a little glass of sherry. Just a weeny one.

Oh! Oh, the telephone ... it's ringing ...

THE GLASS PORCH

•

Patricia Duncker

A married woman decided to leave her husband. She told him about her decision and how she had arrived at her conclusions one Sunday morning over breakfast. Her husband was eating toast in his pyjamas. He went on covering sheets of wholemeal in marmalade as she advanced various explanations, but no compromising excuses.

All right, he said, when she had finished, and how do you propose to support yourself? She stared at him blankly. Face facts, he said, swallowing a mouthful of sugary tea. You do two hours a week of voluntary marriage guidance counselling. And given what you've just been telling me, I hope to God you only listen. You do four hours at the Old People's Home for which you are paid £1.30 an hour. You don't earn a penny for the Red Cross evenings, nor for the young drug addicts' rehabilitation scheme. So your entire weekly income amounts to £5.20. I doubt that would even cover your bus fares. Are you going to tramp down to Women's Aid and say that I've beaten you? You'll have to muster up a few bruises. I suppose you could always fling yourself downstairs. Or are you going to potter off to Social Security and tell them that I crushed your spirit? Sounds poetic, but a bit unrealistic. And I'm not moving out of here just to suit you. You could always go and stay with your sister until you've sorted out that muddle in your head. Mind you, she couldn't even keep you in handkerchiefs. And

19

anyway, you always say she drives you mad with her complaining. Well, why don't you go to your sister's for a week, think it all over and come back next Friday? I can eat at the canteen.

He paused.

I'll give you the money for the train fare, he said peaceably.

But I need, I desire … she thought.

You amount to nothing, he said.

She went upstairs to pack.

He got up to take a bath.

The water was steaming as it belched out of the tap in rushing jerks. He turned the cold tap on as well. He selected two clean towels out of the airing cupboard and added a little Badedas to the incoherent flow. The viscous green trickle began to dissolve into foam, surging round the whirlpools of hot and cold water. He went in search of his transistor with the intention of listening to 'The Archers Omnibus'. He hummed a little tune. The bath was full of foam. He sat down on the lavatory, speculatively. All the familiar objects settled down around him to offer encouragement. His electric razor snuggled into its case, the flannels folded themselves into squares, a small pile of unused scented soaps rearranged itself into the colours of the rainbow, declaring the importance of simple beauties in domestic surroundings. His toothbrush pushed hers to the other side of the glass. A long and satisfying turd slid out of his arse. He eased his buttocks more comfortably against the bowl and looked down at his cock, uncircumcised, neatly shrivelled, hanging into the void. His shit smelled of casual victory. The lavatory paper unrolled towards him in a gesture of comradely confidence. He helped himself to more squares then he would usually use. He felt he deserved it. The bath filled with scented foam. Even the soft, gurgling flush of the cistern as he touched the chrome seemed to shake his hand in congratulation. He lowered his backside gently into the bath. Those first few moments in a hot bath, as the night melts away and the water caresses your skin are always sensual, masterly, reassuring. He leaned back, letting the foam rise up to his ears and sighed with pleasure. He closed his eyes.

She sat on the edge of the bed, her skirt pulled well down over her knees, her eyes fixed on the roses in the wallpaper. The pattern unfolded endlessly across the wall. The roses smelt of putrefaction. She watched the flowers fading, splaying open in thick shafts of sunlight. The house was beginning to curl up and die. In a panic she pulled her small suitcase out of the wardrobe. Then there was a moment of terrible hesitation as she realized that the dresses hanging in the cupboard had begun to rot. They smelt of mushrooms and horse shit. She slammed the door shut and rushed at the chest of drawers. Her vests, underwear and nylon slips were still untainted. Quickly she flung handfuls of brassieres, suspender belts, nylon stockings, carefully darned at the toes, into the bag. Two blouses in the drawer beneath could still be salvaged, but the slow, sweet odour of decomposition had already touched all her cardigans and pullovers. She fled from the room and plunged downstairs. It was becoming more important to escape from the house than to plunder its spoils. She risked the kitchen.

At first glance all was well. The surfaces were wiped clean, the breakfast dishes neatly stacked; but as she stared mistrustfully at the white and cream cupboards she saw a slow brown stain running down one of the doors. A movement startled her. There was something stirring inside the washing machine. She froze. Slowly, the metal circle turned over, once, twice, stopped. She looked around desperately. Every surface was covered in old food, rotten vegetables, plates of Chinese takeaway, abandoned, weeks old, bottles of beer, flat, half-drunk, saucepans filled with inedible, hideous grease, frying pans thick with congealed and rotting sausages. An ashtray overflowing with fag ends stood next to an evil-smelling pot of raspberry jam. The odours mounted up like a pyramid, one upon the other. She clapped her hand to her mouth and backed out of the door. Clearly there was very little time left.

Upstairs, he sank peacefully under the warm foam and then reached for the shampoo. His hair was streaked with grey, but still thick. He squeezed a soggy blob of Wash and Go onto his left hand and gently began to massage his dandruff. His toes rose out of the steam on either side of the taps; a corn bulged on the side of his instep. He surveyed the yellow lump critically. These things happen. He would apply another of those pink corn plasters he had in the medicine cabinet. In time it would drop off.

She went through the pockets of his jacket and helped herself to the fifty pounds left in his wallet that remained after the weekend shopping. Then she took out the credit card and the cheque book. She did not feel safe in the hallway. On the table by the phone there was a pile of used Kleenex which had not been there half an hour before. There was a half-eaten biscuit and a mass of elderly crumbs. She swept up his car keys and risked putting on her old corduroy coat. She had had this coat for years, long before her marriage. It was now her gardening coat, and smelt not of stealthy decomposition but of fresh, green earth. She paused, reinhabiting the coat. One button was missing. Here were her gardening gloves, worn through at the tips, stuffed into the pocket. She put them on. Handbag. Small bag. She burst into the sitting room and snatched her favourite cassettes out of the black semi-circular grid where her husband stored them all in alphabetical order. The sitting room was littered with crisp packets, Coca-Cola cans and newspapers everywhere, on the floor, on the tables, stuffed into the cracks of the armchairs. The cushions sagged greasily onto the carpet. She screwed her eyes to slits and snatched back her music; nothing but dance music, tangos, rumbas, waltzes, galliards, can-cans, minuets, flamenco, gay gordons, country and western, the unadulterated polka. She rammed the music into her bag. The song rang in her head like a mantra. You should see me dance the polka, you should see me cover the ground, you should see my coat-tails flying, as I whirl my partner round. She bolted out of the room.

She stood before the front door wearing her gardening clothes, carrying nothing but her handbag and a small suit-case.

The keys were hanging from the lock on the front door of the house.

The door was locked.

She let herself silently out of the house and shut the door carefully behind her. The Yale clicked into place.

She stood inside the glass porch with the keys in her hand. She looked at the keys. They were her husband's keys. She flung them back through the letter box as if she had been burned.

The glass porch ran the length of the house. It was built on the south side and caught all the sun. They kept the

23

living room curtains pulled shut on hot days, to keep out the heat. There were no geraniums or cacti in the porch. She had wanted to have flowering plants, so that the porch would have been a mass of colour and greenery. He had told her that she couldn't. The glass porch was tiled and bare. She swept the tiles clean every day. At the end of the glass porch was another door, the outside door, the door which led down the garden path by the side of the house past the garage. The outside door was also made of glass, but reinforced glass, glass melted into a strong wire grille, thick, twisted wire to discourage burglars.

And the outside door was always kept locked. She had just slid the keys through the letter box. They were now lying splayed out upon a filthy, flowered carpet.

She was therefore imprisoned within the glass porch.

She stood shaking in the warm bare space, long, clean, unchanging, like a vaginal canal. She tried the outside door, knowing that it was locked. The handle was warm to the touch. She took a deep breath and walked back to the front door. This was a Victorian door in patterned coloured glass, ovals, squares, neat whirling patterns in yellow, burnt red and cobalt blue. The lead divisions, smooth and sure as a draughtsman's lines, maintained the whole. She leaned against the heavy Victorian door. It was firmly locked. She felt the glass gathering heat and force.

Upstairs, he scrubbed his chest with a loofah she had bought at the Body Shop, then sank back, pink, hairy and content. He turned on the radio and watched a little blob of foam sliding down the sticky grille of the transistor. The last hymn of the morning service from St Margaret's, County Antrim poured forth.

She prowled the length of the porch like a panther, carrying her bags. She looked utterly ridiculous.

He sang along with the last verse of the hymn. Praise, my soul, the King of Heaven. They used to sing that at school.

She put down her bags.

He turned on the hot tap.

Suddenly she took off one shoe, and, holding it ferociously by the toe, attacked the marvellous curling glass swirls with her heel. The lead lines gave way as if they had only been pencil marks, the glass fractured and split. She struck and struck, again and again. Huge fragments, tiny splinters, went hurtling into the front hall, covering the oily yellow roses that were rotting on the floor. She yelled in triumph. The entire lead frame shivered and gave way. She recoiled, jubilant, from the gaping hole that hung senseless like a bleeding mouth with all the teeth knocked out. She swung round, and, gathering all her force, attacked the gleaming panes which revealed the stately process of lawns, dug beds and raked gravel. The garden shattered into a thousand elegant diamonds and crumbled before her. Now she knew the absolute pleasure of destruction. Pane after pane shivered and collapsed before her force. Her shining, flaying heels – for she had now removed both her shoes – created huge, circling spider patterns with a bullet hole in the centre of the vibrating cracks. She smashed the glass outwards, away from herself, but inevitably great flying splinters cascaded onto the tiles of the porch. No matter, she was untouchable. Miraculously, her stockinged feet remained undamaged, uncut. She stretched upwards, moving back towards the outside door, and flung herself against the smooth clear sheets of roofing glass which began to pour down, translucent, shining, deadly, solid masses of glass rain.

In his terror he knocks the transistor into the water. The entire house is shaking, heaving, like a woman in labour. Great chunks of glass are falling into the bath; the fluffy blue mat which he had shaken out, not half an hour before, is covered in broken splinters and glass dust. The mirror above the basin has great jagged cracks across the surface. Shards of broken glass are appearing everywhere in the bathroom, on the floor, in the basin, in the lavatory, in the soap dish, on the flannels, all over the window ledge and the wooden shelf with his electric razor in its smooth black case, now covered with a broken mass of glass.

Her right arm strikes, again and again, and with each magnificent, exuberant blow her cup overflows in a mighty torrent of dancing joy.

Upstairs, a man stands, naked and preposterous as St Sebastian. With every move his skin is pierced and bleeding. A thousand tiny flecks of blood are covering his body, every wound a puncture from the flying glass. The blood runs down into the bath, discolouring the foam.

Downstairs, a woman pauses to adjust her coat and scarf. She puts on her shoes. She dusts the splinters from her bag with her gardening gloves. A faint tinkle of fragments falls from the towel rail. Then she steps out through the empty frames of the ruined porch into pure light and fresh, clean autumn air.

RED ROSES FOR A BLUE LADY

•

Christine Harrison

Mrs Stanley's husband kept a signed, silver-framed photograph of Greta Garbo on their bedroom dressing table. He had sent away for it when he was sixteen years old; his first taste of passion, like wild unripe fruit. There had been just two women in his life – Greta Garbo and Mrs Stanley.

Mrs Stanley was large and had beautiful grey eyes. Perhaps the expression on her face was similar to that of Garbo, a certain detachment, an unshareable aloof sensuality, a sort of sadness, as if she lived somewhere else away from her physical body. It was a job to know what Mrs Stanley was thinking – or if she was thinking anything.

The Stanleys had run the local flea-pit cinema, the Grand, for nearly thirty years. It was a family concern. Mr Stanley was projectionist, ticket seller and occasional chucker-out. Mrs Stanley was usherette, ice-cream seller and cleaner. You could spend your whole life cleaning a cinema. All those sweet papers and God knows what.

In the old days there had been a staff. The cinema had been bright and clean then, the floor washed with perfumed disinfectant, the seats unripped. There had been an usherette with a short, Hollywood-style red swirly skirt.

Things had gone downhill. The curtains were full of dust and some of the seats unusable – which did not matter very much as the days of full houses were long past.

Apart from the cleaning, Mrs Stanley rather liked the

27

work. It was second nature to her now. She liked showing people to their seats, flicking her torch on and off. If she sometimes saw more than she bargained for in its bright beam, she did not let it bother her. During the film she sat on a narrow tip-up seat at the back. Day after day of watching successive films must have had something to do with her dreamy expression. It was as if her mind was an empty receiver of impressions.

They had had no friends in all the years of small-town life. Why should they need friends, whose acquaintanceship with Stewart Granger, James Mason, Deborah Kerr was so intimate, every facial expression known, every lift of the eyebrow? Vivien Leigh. Michael Redgrave. With such a company of interesting and beautiful people, so well-dressed, so able to express their emotions – what would you be doing with the neighbours or anyone else in the town?

And they had each other. They knew each other's ways as if they were two blind moles in a tunnel – the knowledge was gained by means of different senses from sight or even sound. They would have been hard put to it to describe each other's appearance, and they did not indulge in conversation for its own sake. Their conversation was minimal and mostly cinematographic.

When Mr and Mrs Stanley chose a film to watch it would almost be like choosing which friend to visit,

'What about Jean Kent dear? We haven't seen her for ages.'

'That would be lovely, she's so vivacious – she does cheer you up.'

Or Glynis Johns or Joan Greenwood or Leslie Howard.

It was always Garbo films for special occasions, a wedding anniversary or a birthday – Mr Stanley would give a private showing in the afternoon, just for the two of them.

Mr Stanley was romantic in ways like this. Always buying her flowers, huge bunches done up in cellophane and ribbons. She never knew what to do with them. They only had the little flat, and they did not spend much time in it. She took to putting the flowers in the cinema foyer, in a couple of old jugs. She ate the chocolates he gave her.

On Saturday they did a children's afternoon. Very few children came to it. They did not like Roy Rogers and Flash Gordon, having already cut their teeth on science fiction and supped on horror videos. The audience for these Saturday shows was a young adult one – Mr Stanley's fare, although he did not realise it, was cult viewing. The older and more crackly the film, the better it was liked. Mrs Stanley, sitting at the back on her tip-up seat, would watch the beam from the projectionist's box as the film spattered into resurrected life, blue cigarette smoke curling and mingling with the beam. She put a chocolate coffee cream into her mouth.

After the Saturday afternoon show the cinema closed for the weekend. Mr Stanley counted up the money (they didn't get very rich on the proceeds, but that hardly came into things) while Mrs Stanley swept up the crisp packets. Saturday night and Sunday they showed films just for their own pleasure. It didn't matter to the Stanleys that Saturday night would have been the best night to stay open. Whose cinema was it, anyway?

Going out into the street after being in the cinema all afternoon was always a shock. In the dark world of the cinema life pulsed, the deep dark emotions, significant meetings and partings, relationships of intense interest. Outside everything was superficial, meaningless. The people hurrying in and out of shops, chatting in the street, had nothing to say of the slightest interest.

And when they emerged after an evening show to the fluorescent lamplight and the night-time riff-raff, on their way to supper at the little café – run by an Italian family – which stayed open until midnight, Mrs Stanley's tiredness, lying on her heavily these days like a carrier bag full of shopping she was unable to put down, distanced everything, the so-called real world, even further – she hardly noticed anything. She ate her egg and chips and her chocolate éclair in a dream.

Then it was time to go home – the flat above the chemist's shop, only a stone's throw from the cinema itself.

They had lived in the same flat since the day they were married. It was all they needed – somewhere to sleep, money-in-the-slot gas fire. The glass-topped coffee table had a fine layer of dust. But in the bedroom the silver-framed picture of Greta Garbo on the kidney-shaped dressing table looked as new as ever.

As they got into bed, pulling the oyster-coloured satin quilt up to their necks in the chilly room, Mr Stanley would say,

'What shall we have next month, Joany?'

'We haven't seen Margaret Lockwood for ages.' Mrs Stanley loved Margaret Lockwood – her wide mouth which would curl up in scorn, her dark flashing eyes. On the whole she preferred women. Except Greta Garbo. Aping about in men's things in that film Mr Stanley said was her best – *Queen Christina* – they must have seen it twenty times if they'd seen it once. And that picture on the dressing table, staring out of the silver frame – she had a silly look, a really silly look. Margaret Lockwood, on the other hand, was the sort you could have had a conversation with, she had opinions, you could see that. Garbo wouldn't have much to say, certainly not to her. Mrs Stanley closed her eyes. She was dreadfully, dreadfully tired. The cinema seemed to get bigger every day when it came to the cleaning of it. It had started to invade her dreams. She was stuck to the floor with chewing gum, she was sweeping up ice-cream wrappers like autumn leaves, she was ankle deep in them.

The following evening, as she sat on her uncomfortable little seat at the back of the cinema, she wondered what was the matter with her. When it came to her time in the month she could feel great clots of blood slip from her. And her legs ached all day long. It wasn't right.

Perhaps she needed a holiday. They never went on holiday. If they had ever felt the need of a change of scene – well, you could go anywhere via the celluloid screen. You could even live for a while in another century, if you felt the ennui of your own.

Mrs Stanley cast about her mind as to what was the matter with her, but she could not find a specific answer. It was just that everything was getting too much for her.

August the third was their wedding anniversary. Thirty-five years. In the afternoon they watched *Gone with the Wind* because *Queen Christina* had not come in time. Mr Stanley had been in a mood about it all day. Mrs Stanley would have enjoyed *Gone with the Wind* if he had not been in such a mood. She preferred Vivien Leigh anyway. In that green velvet gown made, so cleverly, out of curtains, she was far more appealing than Garbo, and Clark Gable was so wild and energetic and had such *savoir-faire*.

Anyway in the evening they had *Ninotchka*.

'Isn't it a bit worn out?' said Mrs Stanley. 'After all, when was it made? 1939?'

But she knew it would never be worn out for him, while he could glimpse that face so strangely special to him. She really thought her husband had an obsession about Garbo. 'That woman' was how Mrs Stanley thought of her. All those pictures lining the cinema stairs – all of them were Garbo. And a huge one in the box office.

They say she ended up living a solitary hermit's life. You could see it in her eyes all along. But Mr Stanley obviously thought a lot of her.

She sometimes thought that her husband had secrets. Secret thoughts.

It was in the middle of *Ninotchka* that Mrs Stanley had a terrible pain – not in her head or her heart, as it happened, but right smack in the middle of her belly.

Mr Stanley, up there in the projectionist's box, could not be expected to know she was writhing about on the floor among the cigarette ends.

'Why didn't you shout out?' he complained frantically as he hurried off to summon the doctor.

And when the doctor came, an ambulance had to be called to take her to hospital. Fibroids had caused a haemorrhage. It accounted for her swollen abdomen, aching legs and her exhaustion.

'You don't need it anyway,' said the doctor, referring to Mrs Stanley's womb. 'It's only so much lumber to you. And while you're about it you should get some of that weight off.' He didn't really have much of a bedside manner – even if he did look like Michael Redgrave. He didn't have that nice voice either. Michael Redgrave's voice was beautiful and thrilling with a little catch in it. And Michael would never have chosen a word like 'lumber' about something that was after all part of oneself, part of being a woman. But she had got fat. And she felt old. And not very well at all and was glad to get into a hospital bed and have a rest. When the auxiliaries cleaned the big wards, she was thankful there was something the matter with her and she could just lie in bed and watch.

She had her operation, and Mrs Stanley's womb was incinerated. It went up in smoke.

A large bouquet of flowers arrived. 'With love from George' – that was Mr Stanley's name. Mr Stanley himself did not appear at visiting time for several days. The hospital was on the outskirts of town and quite a long bus ride away. And there was the cinema. He had not closed it, and was managing on his own. And illness made him nervous. When he at last got round to visiting his wife, it was like venturing out into the veldt. And as he walked down the hospital corridor, trying to make no sound, as if he wasn't there, he had an apprehensive air of suspicion at this new environment. He tried to hide behind the large bunch of flowers he was carrying. He sat on the edge of the chair beside her bed.

'Red roses,' he said, 'for a blue lady,' placing the cellophane-wrapped roses on the starched bed cover.

But Joan Stanley had never felt less blue. She felt unreasonably happy. She could not remember when she had had such a good time as in the past few days. She scarcely noticed her post-operative aches and pains.

She did not mind that he did not stay long. It was as if she had emerged, not simply from an anaesthetic, but from a deep coma.

And this unaccountable happiness was not in any way a drugged euphoria, it was something simple, deep and satisfying. It was also a light thing. She was dipping her finger in a real world. She laughed a lot. She felt an undercurrent of something she thought was called joy. It was delightful.

It was something about being in this ward of women. It

was real, satisfying and soothing. There was something about their women's lot that drew them together. They were so drily amusing, so uninhibited, even vulgar; so real. These women, who had experienced childbirth, menstrual troubles and now the removal or repair of their wombs, had a camaraderie, not quite as soldiers who had suffered together, not quite as prisoners who had relinquished their freedom, but as the ones it was all done to, the broken ground from which bloody life springs – who knew the whispered secret of it all. And although Mrs Stanley's womb was lost and had never been inhabited, she felt herself, nevertheless, one of this company of women. The secret was in their slightly raucous laughter and in the way they looked at each other gently. They were indulgent and tender with each other, just for now, knowing that it would not last.

The woman in the next bed was a farmer's wife called Iris. She had two grown-up sons who came to see her, big men with farm workers' hands, calloused, the earth never quite scrubbed away from under the nails. They brought bunches of flowers from their cottages. They held their babies on one knee with one huge hand. In the bed on the other side was Mary, a beautiful young woman with long dark hair, whose husband came to visit her on alternate nights to her lover. It all made Mr Stanley uneasy on his brief visits.

Then on the day before Mrs Stanley was due to come out, she was looking at a magazine that Mary had passed to her. In it there was this picture of Greta Garbo. She must have been sixty years old, or seventy even. She was swimming in the sea, and all you saw in the picture was her head above the water. Just this expanse of shimmering sea water and in the middle of it, like John the Baptist's head on a silver plate, was Garbo's head, hair tucked into a severe helmet-like bathing hat. It was a very odd picture and Mrs Stanley cut it out of the magazine. She did not know quite why she wanted to keep it. She put it in her locker. The following day she went home in a taxi.

Over the next few days she tried very hard to fall back into her old life. Mr Stanley was glad she was back. He had swept the cinema himself, managed everything. And he had ordered *Brief Encounter* for Mrs Stanley's first visit to the cinema. He knew how much she liked Celia Johnson and Trevor Howard, how they were almost like her own flesh and blood.

He sat her at the back of the cinema, and tucked a rug around her and gave her a packet of marshmallows. Then he went off to the projectionist's box.

Mrs Stanley enjoyed the film but somehow could not get quite as engrossed as she had been the countless times she had seen it before. She noticed how good the acting was, and the love story did not fail to move her, but she didn't actually cry very much – just a couple of tears, that was all. But she was glad it wasn't a Garbo film.

For some reason she had taken to carrying the picture of Garbo about with her – it was folded in her cardigan pocket now. It was like a talisman, as if it might work some charm. It was burning a hole in her cardigan pocket.

It was all leading up to something, she had an unmistakable feeling that it was. She felt driven.

As they stood one evening in the foyer, Mr Stanley fussing about doing one or two last-minute things before locking up, she took the picture out of her pocket.

'Who do you think that is?' she asked Mr Stanley, showing him the photograph, smoothing it out, the severed-looking head floating on the sea, the harsh Nordic features, the gimlet-eyed Garbo. It was the face of a mediaeval knight who had spent long years in the Crusades and seen so many dreadful things that now the world held out no hope for happiness. It had a look of stoic suffering which disdained despair.

'It's Greta Garbo,' said Mrs Stanley. 'That's who it is.'

Mr Stanley looked at the photograph. At once she wished she had not shown it to him, but it was too late, it was done.

He looked so suddenly abandoned and hopeless, so suddenly old, his face puckering in a strange way. His whole body seemed to go limp as if a spring inside him had been broken.

'We've run out of choc ices,' he said, 'I must leave a note to order some more,' and he went off. He didn't come back for a long time. And when he did Mrs Stanley could see that she had done something irrevocable.

Well – what on earth had she expected? Had she thought he would say, 'Old age has not been kind to her,' or 'she was only human, you know,' or even, 'yes, my dearly beloved inscrutable face is still there, I can still see it'?

No. He had taken it very hard. He would never recover from seeing that severed head. How cruel she was. How stupid! To want him to give up his fantasy.

How unreasonable and unkind to want, after all these years, to have the woman decapitated for good.

MUSTARD

•

Catherine Merriman

Where d'you get mustard, seven o'clock Friday evening, in the back-of-beyond Welsh countryside? Hell and blast. The village shop is closed. When isn't it? The yob at the garage is apologetic. Got petrol, sir, he says, but no mustard. A comedian. Mrs. Crabb by the chapel, who cleans the cottage, has got mustard but won't give me any. Just picked up her half-squeezed tube of it and simpered, 'Well I can't really give you any of this, Mr T, can I?' Yes you could, you cretinous woman, I thought, you could squeeze some into an egg cup and give it to me. But I didn't say it, because her idiocy paralysed me, and I can't go back there now. Shame Mrs Crabb isn't Welsh, bet any of the other villagers would have offered me the whole tube. And then bellyached about it afterwards, but who cares. I'd have got it.

So why do I need mustard, seven o'clock Friday evening? Well, I need it to go with that enormous steak, a good pound-weighter, that's sitting, dripping deliciously, in the kitchen fridge. The steak that I bought this afternoon, in a small town somewhere off the M4 where nobody knows me, and which I have to eat, and destroy the evidence of eating, before eleven tonight. That's when Miranda's taxi will arrive from the station, after her working dinner in Bristol. And I cannot eat it, I will not eat it, without mustard. The crime must be perfect.

I suppose I could try the Little Chef, back down on the

main road. Order a coffee, and nick some of their mustard sachets by the till. Or do they have those obscene squidgy yellow tomatoes on the tables? Would one of those fit in a pocket? Anyway, it's a forty-minute round trip. Oh Christ.

It seems extraordinary that we don't have mustard here, in the cottage store cupboard. But I've just checked again and we don't. God knows we use enough at home, to flavour all those disgusting lentil soups.

The stupid cow wears leather, of course. Ho ho. She eats cheese, drinks milk, wears leather. 'How d'you think they produce milk?' I've asked her. 'What d'you suggest they do with all the little baby boy calves the cows give birth to, so you can have your precious milk and cheese? Sell them as pets? Return them to the wild?'

Miranda becomes sulky when she's forced to rationalise her vegetarianism. She's too lazy to go the whole hog – my, I am witty tonight – and become a vegan, and anyway she thinks it's cranky. Sandals and beads and back-to-the-earth New Ageism; not her scene at all. And all her women friends are vegetarian, it's practically *de rigeur* these days.

I should have stood up for myself years ago. Men need meat. It's lack of meat that makes us wimps. Welshmen eat meat. Look at all the bloody sheep. They're not ashamed of rearing meat. What else could they farm on all these sodding mountains? Something pretty for people like Miranda? Tulips, maybe? Shifty-faced Tucker now, at the bottom of the lane, he gets meat every day. Thinks we're mad. Meat every day, roast beef on Sunday, all on less than 200 quid a week. And look at us, fifty thou a year between us, no kids, a flat in London and a cottage in Wales, and we live on lentils and beans. How times change.

Why should I care whether Miranda knows about the steak? Hell, I'm not frightened of her. But it's the subversiveness that appeals. I shall enjoy it more, marinated in deceit. Oh I shall. But I must have mustard.

Tucker. He'd have it. That roast beef. And he owes us. All those cheeses we gave his dopey wife a fortnight ago, after we'd had the Simpsons down – a dollop of mustard'd be the least we deserve. Dolcelatte, Cambozola, a great wedge of that god-awful Gruyère. Miranda took them down to the farmhouse in a basket, Lady Bountiful in green wellingtons, picking her way through the mud and muck and his pack of belly-crawling sheepdogs. Pressed them on Mrs Tucker. 'Oh but we absolutely insist, I'm sure the village shop doesn't run to Dolcelatte, such a shame to think of food wasted.' We could have taken them back to London with us. But no, Miranda says, they'll stink the car out. Liar. She was just struck on impressing the natives.

I'll go down there now. And this time take an egg cup. Be prepared.

Christ, that's better. I say it myself, I'm a mean chef. A pound of rare steak. Black pepper and mustard. Mangetout and cucumber salad. Three – just three – new potatoes. Two glasses of burgundy. Ah, burgundy. What's the point of red wine without red meat? Oh, bliss.

That Tucker though. Ha! Wait till I tell Miranda. A nasty sense of humour lurks in that dour shell. Nasty, but delicious. For a man of few words he picks them well. Opened the door to me himself. Stared at the egg cup while I explained. 'Ay,' he nodded, 'The missus'll have some mustard,' and disappeared inside. Didn't take the egg cup. Left me standing there, the lunatic from London proffering his dinky begging bowl. Returned with an unopened jar and handed it over, dismissed my thanks. Then walked down to the yard gate with me, as if he didn't trust me to close it properly.

How did he get the subject round to those cheeses? God knows. But he did. He and the missus only eat cheddar, he told me. They gave the cheeses to the dogs. But never again, he said. 'Do make 'em fart,' he said. 'Fart something chronic.' Our food, not even fit for dogs. Hell, and he kept a straight face. They know how to slap you down, hats off to them.

I admire him. With a pound of red meat inside me, I can admire him. Fire and spirit. Flesh and blood. Sly bugger. Ready with the needle like that. Ah, that's what meat does for you. The war engine stoked with real fuel. Can't wait to tell Miranda. In fact, can't wait to see her. Roll on bedtime. She's sleeping with a carnivore tonight.

A STEP AWAY FROM TROUBLE

•

Catherine Merriman

On my way up to Clive's in Brynmawr I stop off at the Corn Exchange pub in Gilwern. I've got a spare helmet on the back of the XS because I half-expect Bethan to need a lift, but she isn't here; her brother Kev must have taken her in the van.

I try not to notice Doggy, hunched over a glass the far end of the bar. It's only nine-thirty and he looks stewed already. He walked out on his wife Rose three months ago but the bachelor life don't seem to be bringing him joy.

As I order my pint I'm aware he's sidling up to me. He's on the whisky and his eyes are mean. He stares at me.

'Surprised you aren't screwing Rose too,' he says nastily.

I reckon I've come in at the tail end of a conversation he's having with the whisky.

'Ta,' I say with a polite smile, 'But I prefer to roll my own.'

Doggy scowls; he wants to have it both ways and feel insulted that I haven't screwed his wife, but isn't quite smashed enough. He soon will be, though, and I'm out tonight to enjoy myself, so I down my pint fast.

The encounter's still niggling me as I pull out on to the Heads of the Valleys road, and instead of going straight to Brynmawr I decide to cut up through Llanelly Hill and take a detour to Blaenavon. Drop in on Rose. No carnal motives, mind – just to spite Doggy and say howdo to a mate. Why shouldn't she have callers? Miserable bastard, Doggy is.

It's a clear dry night – asking for the scenic route. I power up through the beechwoods to the Hill and take a left on to the Blaenavon road. Over a thousand foot up here, and it's a lost world – grassed-over spoil tips and hummocky workings, derelict sheds, lonely strips of run-down terraces. At night the bike lights funnel you through the blackness. I take the Whistle Inn straight so fast the cattle grid's just a sizzle in my spine.

Then I'm at the Big Pit tourist signs and slowing down for Blaenavon. I cut into the back streets across the main road – Rose's flat is on the eastern slopes, half a hillside above the centre of town. I trundle the bike through the steep narrow roads, past a line of lockups and prop it by the main entrance of the flats. Hers is first floor front. It seems to be in darkness but I ring the bell anyway.

She's in; I see a moon face checking at the window, and then the door buzzes open. Bike boots make a helluva clomp up concrete stairs. Rose's on the landing outside her door in bare feet, cycling shorts and a baggy T-shirt. Had a laid-back day, lucky girl.

'Hiya,' she says, waving me into the flat. None of the lights are on but I can hear the telly in the sitting room. She says she's conserving power because she's only got one token left for the meter, and she must catch 'Cell Block H' at midnight.

It takes me a moment in the gloom to see she's got company. On the leatherette settee there's a pair of gleaming white thighs, shifting position.

'This is Tanya,' Rose says. 'From up the road.'

'Hi,' I say. I've found a face, round and puddingy.

'Hi,' says Tanya. 'Anyone else outside?' She tucks her feet in under her bum so I can sit down.

'Er, nope.' I assume she's asking if I'm an advance party.

My eyes are adjusting to the gloom. Tanya's wearing a dark low-cut top that shows her bra straps and a short tight skirt. She's got a pretty smile.

Rose passes round ciggies and a bottle of Thunderbird and curls up in her armchair. 'She means her old man.' She shakes her head. 'No one there, Tanya, honest.'

'Just let him try,' Tanya says with feeling. 'Bastard.' She grins at me. 'I'm cooling off, don't mind me. I go back there now, I'd cut his sodding balls off.'

Neither of them explains further, they just take swigs of Thunderbird, so after a minute I say, 'I'm on my way to Clive's. Thought I'd drop by.'

'What you done with Bethan then?' Rose asks.

'Gone with Kev.'

Rose nods several times over her ciggy. 'I like Bethan, I do. His girl,' she says to Tanya. She wags the ciggy at me. 'You got a great girl there, you know that? Best you've had. You treat her right, okay?'

Since school Rose has been telling me to treat my girlfriends right. I grin at her and pull on my cigarette.

We watch the adverts in the middle of 'News at Ten'. When they end Tanya loses interest in the telly and turns to me. 'Is that Clive's in Brynmawr?' she asks. 'Party, is it?'

'Kind of. Clive's birthday.'

'Ooh, fancy a party, I do.' Tanya shivers her front with enthusiasm. Shit, I hadn't noticed before, she's got tits like torpedoes.

'Go on then,' Rose urges. 'That'd show 'im. Hey, he'd be mad.' They both start cackling and snorting like I'm not there. I'm fond of Rose but listening to them I feel my sympathies dividing.

Rose stops cackling and pushes at my knee. 'You'll take her, won't you? Just a lift. Go on. Time she had some fun.'

'Ah go on,' begs Tanya.

'Course he will,' says Rose. 'Do a favour for a mate, won't you?'

'Or a mate of a mate,' Tanya sniggers, and they both fall about again.

Seems like the decision's been made. Reckon they've been at the Thunderbird a while. I shrug and say okay. Hell, it's just a ride.

Tanya doesn't want to hang around now and once we've finished our ciggies she's up, tugging on a red fringed jacket.

Rose gets up too. 'He's got a big bike,' she says, grinning at Tanya. 'You hang on tight.'

'Ooh, I will.' Tanya gives me a coy look but I don't flatter myself I've earned it. I reckon it's free to anyone who's not her old man.

She has to nip to the lav on the way out. Rose goes in with her and I hear them whispering and giggling. Rose spends more time in lavs with girlfriends than any woman I know.

Outside the flats I give Tanya the spare helmet, start the XS and flip the rear footrests down. Tanya clutches at the hem of her skirt and squeals, 'How'm I gonna sit on that!' But she does, I don't look round to see how. Just feel those tits ramming into my back, and her arms tight round my waist.

Rose waves us goodbye. I weave the bike back past the lockups, and up to the first junction.

As we round the corner I see a big bloke in singlet and tattoos striding towards us. Determined-looking fella. I've an instant intuition about him.

He stops, bellows, 'Oi!', and lunges into the road. Looks a fit bastard too. Tanya shrieks into my left ear but I've already twisted the grip, and the bloke's just a blur in the scenery.

A hundred yards down the road I ease off and look back. He's given up on us and is making for Rose's flat. His fists are pumping at his sides.

'It's okay,' shouts Tanya in my ear, 'They get on fine, honest. I told Rose if he turned up just to tell him I've gone to Clive's.'

Oh great, I think sourly. I wonder if he knows exactly where Clive's house is. And what transport he's got. Still, nothing'll catch us over the five miles to Brynmawr.

It's a quick left and right, smart left again at the garage at the edge of town, and then we're back out on open road. I crank up the revs. Somewhere along the Whistle straight Tanya slides her hands into my jacket pockets but I reckon it's just to keep them warm. Then we're round the Racehorse Pub bends, and getting a great view of Brynmawr as we drop down off the mountain. Lit up like orange fairyland.

In the town itself we stop off at the off-licence to pick up booze. Tanya wants another bottle of Thunderbird but I say no: I won't allow glass inside jackets on my bike, and I've a cluster of fancy scars on my breastbone to remind me why. So she buys two cans of cider and I get four of Newcastle Brown.

Clive's place is only a short ride on. We turn into his road and see a small crowd on the pavement outside his house. As we trundle up I recognise Kev and Gwynfor, and yeah, the lad with long straggly hair is Clive himself. Funny – for some reason he seems to be trying to kick his own front gate in.

I pull the bike in opposite the house next to a GPZ that must be Jonno's. Beyond it is Gwynfor's trail bike and a few others. Tanya climbs off the XS and after I've propped it we cross the road. Looks like Kev and Gwynfor are try-ing to calm Clive down. Shit, I dunno; first Doggy, then

Tanya, now Clive; I get the feeling I'm only a step away from trouble tonight.

'What's the gate done?' I ask Kev. Gwynfor's nearer but I'm looking for an answer this side of midnight so I pass on him. The gate's only a white wicket, looks harmless enough, but it's got Clive really riled.

'He's mad at Jonno,' says Kev. 'The bastard's done a runner. We were getting in the mood down the road,' he nods towards the lights of a pub on the corner, 'and Jonno's got us all banned. Smashing ashtrays. Tosser.'

Getting banned from your local's no joke. 'Course, it isn't Jonno's local, or Kev's or Gwynfor's. But it is Clive's. No wonder he's steaming. The gate's holding its own, only one rail broken, you have to admire it. Mind you, most of Clive's kicks aren't connecting because he's so pissed. He's wearing a flash cowboy shirt, I notice, grey and burgundy with pearl popper studs. Bet it's a birthday present.

Clive swings round. He's just realised we've arrived.

'Where's the fucker?' he spits, weaving from side to side, as if he thinks maybe Jonno's hiding behind us. Shit, he looks wild.

'Forget him,' Kev says soothingly. He puts an arm round Clive's shoulders. 'You got a party inside. We'll sort it in the morning.'

Clive flings Kev's arm off. 'Fucker!' he bellows. He's shaking – he's going to hit someone soon, for definite. Kev's a brave lad – he's only slight but he's keeping right in there, calm as an undertaker.

Tanya's on tiptoes beside me, waving over the hedge to someone at the front window of the house. It's Marie, Clive's girlfriend. Shit, I think, remembering Tanya's old man. Looks like the girls are mates. Doubt the bloke's going to need directions.

Clive's got his fists up. Gwynfor tries to smother them in a waltzing hug but gets pushed away.

Kev sighs and says, 'You want to hit someone, Clive?'

'Fucking right I wanna hit someone,' roars Clive. 'Gonna fucking kill 'em.'

'Come on then.' Kev lifts his fists and squares up to him. 'Let's fight, Clivey.'

I tug Tanya back a pace. I'm not worried for Kev; he's little but he's strong, and sober. Nor for Clive, because Kev's just humouring him and won't follow anything through.

Clive takes a swing at Kev ferocious enough to lift him off his feet, but it's signposted from the start and Kev only has to step aside to take it on the shoulder padding of his jacket. Then he nips in fast while Clive's recovering and clocks him a sneaky one on the nose.

'Ah fuck,' grunts Clive. He fumbles at his face. Blood looks like gravy under street lights and there's a trickle of it oozing through his fingers.

'Mind your shirt,' says Kev quickly.

'My shirt,' wails Clive. He looks down, instantly forgetting the fight. He starts wrenching at the pearl poppers. Kev helps him get the shirt off, but it's too late. There's a couple of dark splodges down the front.

'Marie gave it me,' moans Clive.

'It's okay,' says Kev. 'We'll soak it. Cold water, no problem.' He unlatches the gate, which only sighs a little on its hinges, and steers Clive up the path towards the front door.

The rest of us follow. I hear Gwynfor introducing himself to Tanya and wonder how long it'll take her to escape. Gwynfor talks like he rides: throttle set on drone, only brakes when the road runs out.

Kev takes Clive into the kitchen to soak the shirt and the rest of us go through to the sitting room. Bethan's on the sofa chatting to Marie; Jaz and Mitch and a few others are over by the drinks. Jaz is rolling a party joint on the table with a dozen skins. I prop myself on the arm of the sofa and tap Bethan on the shoulder with a beer can.

She looks up, smiles, 'Oh hi, great,' and swivels to take the can. 'You heard? We all got booted out the pub. Because of that prat Jonno. Clive's raving.'

'Yeah,' I say, snapping open a can myself. 'I know.' I take a swig. Bethan's in jeans and a black shirt, knotted at the front. You can tell she's Kev's sister. Same small neat shape, same easy calm about her. I want to sink on to the sofa beside her but I can't, with Tanya's old man on my mind.

It looks like Tanya's only just detached herself from Gwynfor's life history. She's pretending to admire bike rally stickers by the window but really she's keeping an eye out.

Reluctantly I push myself up from the sofa and walk over to her.

'Waiting for your old man?' I say over her shoulder.

She glances back at me with a quick smile. I reckon she's regretting coming here already.

'Who's he going to be mad at?' I ask. 'You or me?'

She dips her smile. 'You, maybe. But he don't know you. I won't let on.'

'Would he know the bike?' I ask. I'd heal, but the XS wouldn't.

She thinks. 'Doubt it. Dark, wasn't it. Not to be sure, anyways.'

'What's he drive?'

'Red pickup.'

I nod, and decide not to move the bike.

Clive comes in barechested with Kev behind him. Marie jumps up crying, 'Where's your shirt?' and Kev assures her it's fine, hanging clean as new, just a bit wetter, over the bath. Clive's nose looks puffy and he's still breathing heavy but Jaz has just finished constructing the twelve-skin spliff and presents it to him with a flourish. Kev offers a light and we all sing a round of 'Happy Birthday to you' as Clive gets the joint glowing. That'll mellow him some.

When the singing's over Kev takes me to one side.

'Don't let Jonno in if he comes back. Don't want Clive set off again.'

'You expecting him?' I ask.

'Has to get his bike sometime. Depends if he's still mad. Clive clipped him one outside the pub.'

I glance over at Tanya, and tell Kev we might have another visitor. And why.

'Shit,' murmurs Kev. He thinks about it, and then shrugs. 'Just don't let him near Clive. Sort it outside, okay?'

I nod and return to Tanya, who's still gazing out the window.

'If he turns up, how 'bout you going out to him?' I say. 'Clive's a bit wound up. You want to go back with him, don't you?'

She pulls a face, then sighs and says, 'Suppose so. Yeah.' She points at the window. 'There is someone out there. Not me old man, but some bloke. Across the road.'

I take a look. A big-shouldered lad in a leather jacket is standing by the bikes. Shaved head, fleshy face, long black-and-white tasselled scarf.

'It's Jonno.' Shit, I think. Doesn't look as if he's planning an entrance though. He's trying to pull his GPZ out from the other bikes. But making a mess of it, because he's so pissed. Only a pillock like Jonno would try to ride his bike rat-arsed. He pulls the GPZ a yard out of the line, then seems to give up and lets it roll back. He digs around in his pockets, swaying as he rummages. He's found a packet of fags and he's lighting up. For a moment he seems to be thinking mighty thoughts, face tilted skywards, pulling on the ciggy. Then he recollects himself, works his way out from the bikes and starts walking towards the house.

'Tell Kev,' I say quickly to Tanya. 'Discreet like.' I'm already moving to the door.

I let myself out the front and close the door behind me. Jonno's trying to open the garden gate but it's sulking now and refusing to let him in. He punches it, swearing, jettisons his ciggy, and starts to climb over it.

'Oi!' I call. 'No need to bother. Just piss off, okay.'

'Where's that fucker Clive?' Jonno says thickly. There's a sound of cracking wood as he makes it over the gate. That's another strut gone. Hell, I sigh, walking down to him, and I'm a peaceloving bloke.

I grasp him by his upper arm and swing him round so he's pointing back the way he's come. There's nothing wrong with the gate latch – Jonno just never found it – so I lift it and yank the gate wide. Behind us I hear the front door open – it's Kev and Tanya. I try to push Jonno out on to the pavement but he's seen the others and they're distracting him.

'You get Clive,' he shouts over his shoulder at them. 'Tell him Jonno's here.'

Kev runs down to us and together we shove him through the gate. He's flailing around but nothing purposeful.

'Go home Jonno,' hisses Kev. 'Clive don't want to see you.'

'Get his keys first,' I say. 'He was trying to pull his bike out.'

We both try to find the keys but leather jackets have too many pockets and Jonno's dead set against the idea, swearing and hitting us off.

We're still wrestling with him as headlights approach from down the road. Double headlights, high and wide. We stop wrestling. Oh shit, I think. Could be a pickup.

It is a pickup. A red one. It pulls up twenty yards away and the driver jumps out. The bloke's got a denim jacket on now over his singlet and he's so keen to say hello he leaves the driver's door swinging wide.

Kev, Jonno and I watch him approach, kind of mesmerised. Kev and I because we know who he is and our brains are log-jammed, and Jonno because he's so pissed it's his resting state anyway.

Suddenly Tanya's between me and Jonno. She's slipping her arm around Jonno's waist. Planting a big kiss on his ugly mug. Kev and I come to our senses at the same time, twig what she's doing, and step away. Ooh you clever girl, I think.

Jonno's overjoyed to be so irresistible, flinging his arms around Tanya and trying to stick his tongue in her ear. Such spontaneous affection, it's a pleasure to watch. Even Tanya's old man is smiling. Kind of.

Tanya wriggles away from Jonno, says, 'Ta for a lovely evening,' and skips off towards the pickup.

Tanya's old man stands with his legs braced in front of Jonno, glares at him, and then wallops him a backhander across the face. Jonno never saw it coming and looks surprised more than hurt. So the bloke belts him again and this time Jonno's legs give way and he's down, hard, on his bum. I feel a mite sorry for him, sitting there looking dull on the pavement, but if anyone deserves it he does, and Tanya's old man has come a long way to get satisfaction. It's not his fault he's got the wrong lad.

Kev's tensing, just in case the bloke's a psycho, but I'm fairly sure he's not, and I'm right: he backs off, lifting his palms to us, and says, 'Personal matter, boys. No offence.'

Kev relaxes, and I nod and say, 'None taken'. While Jonno's still wondering who cut his legs off Kev squats down beside him, digs around in his pockets, and finds the bike keys. So Tanya's old man's done Jonno a favour really – he won't be killing himself or anyone else driving home. Done favours all round, in fact.

The bloke strolls back to his pickup. I can see Tanya inside the cab and she don't look scared. Scared women don't titivate in driving mirrors. Reckon we don't need to worry about her.

The pickup roars off up the road. We try to get Jonno on his feet but he's lost interest in being vertical and twists away from us. He pats at the pavement as if it's a lumpy mattress and tries to get his head down. Nothing like a near view of the floor when you're pissed to make you want to stay there. But we can't leave him on the pavement so Kev nips down to his van, reverses it up close, and we heave him into the back. Jonno curls up cosy on the carpet and he's snoring like a two-stroke before we get the back doors closed.

Kev parks the van down the road again and we tramp back into the house. Metallica's on the stereo and the air's sweet and thick. Clive's so mellow now he's fast asleep on the carpet in front of the fireplace. A friendly arm-wrestling contest's going on down the room and Marie and another girl are dancing by the window, heads on each other's shoulders, movements slow and boozy.

I finally get to sink down next to Bethan on the sofa, snap open another beer can, and start mellowing out myself.

A PLACE IN WALES

•

Clare Morgan

'It's out there. I know it is.'

The rhythmical squeak of the spinning wheel stuttered and slowed, the oscillating arc of its shadow on the farther wall came to a stop.

'You're imagining things,' said the woman, and cupped her two hands, one over each of her kneecaps, and eased the tension out of the back of her neck, and sat quite relaxed, her shoulders leaning slightly forward over her knees and her backbone curved so that you could see the diminishing knots of her vertebrae spoiling the smooth line of her shirt.

'You're tired, I expect. You've had a bad day. Why don't you go up to bed?'

The man waved away her suggestion and twisted irritably in his chair by the fire. He was a young man, younger than the woman, quite considerably younger. The firelight reflected on the flesh of his neck made him seem younger still, the skin so smooth and shiny, like a child's. He could almost have been her son, or perhaps a nephew, the single issue of some older sister.

He picked up the poker and dabbled the end of it into the red-hot spaces between the coals. Although it was late April and the air outside was warm enough to be comfortable without a coat, he had insisted on a fire, on the grounds that the stone of which the old house was made gave off its own persistent chill.

The woman had acquiesced without saying anything, watching him get the twigs together and arrange them in the grate, watching him select little bits of coal, not so big that the twigs would burn out before the coal ignited, not so small they would be unable to form the core of the larger fire it was in his mind to build. There had been a moment, as there is with all fires, when she scarcely expected it to light, thought that the small flame sucking in air from underneath as it struggled up the side of the first twig would surely flicker and extinguish. But it had taken hold, and he had turned and smiled at her, there on his knees in front of the grate, a smile of triumph, a smile of satisfaction which forgot everything else, a smile contained in its own network of order, its own regularity of cause and effect, a child's smile which occurs so rarely in the faces of grown-up men and women, and when it does is apt to blind those about them with its purity.

The woman had smiled back, adult and mechanical, a smile which stopped before it started, the brief shadow of it in her head reflected by the even briefer representation on her lips. Then she had left him to his fire and gone purposefully about the remainder of her day, making lists and ticking things off as she accomplished them, watching the hands of the clock revolve the hours around her, watching the light change shape, registering somewhere in her head how the mountains which surrounded the farmhouse grew denser as the sun slewed past the south and began its descent to the sea.

It was strange how, after rain, everything seemed very black. It had rained that morning at about ten o'clock, a brief, hard shower which drummed on the roof and the earth and the backs of her hands as she reached for the latch of the casement window and pulled it to with a definite click.

'Why don't you leave it open?' he had said, coming into the kitchen with a plate with crumbs on it and an earthenware mug in which she could just see the dregs of one of his bitter, concocted drinks.

His special drinks irritated her. She thought, why did I have to marry a man who drinks green China tea? Then felt guilty about it almost at once because at least his drinks gave him something to think about, aromatic infusions whose presence filled the kitchen and seeped through the house, she could smell them clinging in the upstairs curtains, and scenting his breath when he came towards her.

She remembered his insistence on the fire and said nothing and left the window shut knowing that would be a statement in itself and doubting he would challenge it. She didn't really care. Her mind was already taken up with the blackening hills as the rain swept across them, grey bands of matter, specks of steel, great clumps of stuff deposited there at the blind end of the valley as though the opening of the clouds was part of some barely perceived but definite metaphysical intention.

She remembered the first time she had driven up the valley (it had been early October and the whole place was fiery with dying bracken). The thought had come to her, perhaps I shall find God here, which was a very strange thought because she had always, as far as she knew, been an atheist. But she had never thought it again and had not let it bother her, because that is the effect a radical change of place can have on you. It can do peculiar things to the usual balance of your mind, subvert the basis of the ideas you hold and always have held, knowing by logical deduction that they are right.

The next time she had driven up the valley was when they came for good. She didn't think about God this time, and the hills were particularly black. When you got out of the car the wind was enough to knock you over. Although it was only early afternoon, the light was already diminishing. She wondered why they had come.

But the next day the sun was out and the air was pleasantly crisp and the waterfall which you could hear constantly through the kitchen window made patient noises. Her husband had seemed enthusiastic. They made plans for spring bulbs, and hens (six of them) and argued, not very seriously, about the merits of keeping a cockerel. Cockerels were so fine-looking. She imagined one strutting about the yard with his comb all red and glistening and his beak yellow and shiny and his 'cock-a-doodle-doo' so clear and pure it would reach the very tips of the hills and glance off them on its way out into space.

When she said this to her husband they both laughed. It was still in her head, them both laughing, and she took it out occasionally and looked at it, how their bodies swayed in towards each other and out again, with their heads thrown back and their eyes half-closed, and the sound of it rising like colourless smoke. He had probably touched her. She thought she remembered the roughish feel of the hairs on the back of his hand. But she could not be sure.

In any case the cockerel had been decided against, it would make too much noise and possibly distract him, certainly would when he eventually got down to work. And the hens themselves, nothing had come of them, the hen house needed attention and neither of them knew what to do. Nor had they got around to planting the bulbs. She had bought a few, a dozen in a white paper bag one day when she went shopping, but they were still there, in the back of the kitchen drawer, sprouting no doubt, she didn't dare put her hand all the way in in case she touched them, shoots of things were so pale and fleshy, and the granular feel of them against her fingers' ends was sure to make her shudder.

Nor had her husband ever actually got down to work. The first week, they had set up a table in the small room at the far end of the bedroom, tucked under a corner of the eaves. They had laid in supplies of paper, and she had carefully put out a new pencil (in the only colour he would use, a deep, bright red) and a new silvery sharpener beside it, knowing how he said he could never write unless his pencil was sharp. At the end of November she added a paraffin heater and put up curtains to keep out the midwinter wind. She thought perhaps he might find he wanted to write at night. She dusted his typewriter. But nothing had come of it. He occasionally went to the room and stayed there for an hour. She could hear him pacing, and once she caught him smuggling his radio up the stairs.

She told him not to be too disappointed, that it would take time to get back to things, to really recover. He didn't seem to listen, grew increasingly morose and spent hours walking up and down watching the waterfall carving its grey, curvilinear basin out of the stone. He became more reluctant to take his daily pills. He said,

'Pills! What have pills ever created but this vacuum in my head?'

She had to watch him closely to make sure he didn't just pretend to take them and hide them under his tongue and spit them surreptitiously into the sink. Once he said,

'It's living here. It's the silence. It won't let me think.'

But when they had driven back over the border, and the familiar Englishness of things had closed over them, the fields and the hedges and the dirty grass verges spangled with fragments of black plastic bags, he had said he felt claustrophobic, and they spent a restless couple of days trying the patience of a long-suffering friend.

For a week he seemed glad to be back. He spent much more time shut up in the little room, and she actually thought he might be writing. It was at this time that she bought the spinning wheel, second hand, and a greasy fleece, and set up her own space in the corner of the big living room right at the far end away from the fire, just near enough to the window so that if she held her head at the correct angle she could see out. He hadn't been pleased, and told her he thought it was a waste of time.

'Spinning,' he said. 'What's the point? Nowadays it's all done for you.'

But she said she found it relaxing, and time was something they both had plenty of. So she persevered and soon became quite expert, so that at first nearly every evening and then for quite significant parts of the day too you would find her seated at the spinning wheel and bowing her back to the rhythm of its steady revolution.

Her husband spent more and more time watching her. He seemed angry, but fascinated. It was as if he watched against his will. He was fascinated by the way she drew out the yarn, how the yarn drew out and out until there was miles of it hanging in skeins about the place like ropey cobwebs. The smell of it went up his nose and into the centre of his head until he became convinced the last thing on earth he would be aware of, at that one culminating moment when the soul leaves the body and the human relic casts itself into the nerveless abysses of eternity, the very last thing would be the smell of freshly-spun wool, and the rapid twist of his wife's white fingers, blind and hideless as baby snakes.

He didn't bother to go up to the little room now. The

papers on the desk grew damp and bent up at the edges
and dust settled into the curves the bent-up edges made.
She didn't like going into that room any more. It had that
emptiness about it you get when someone has died. Absence,
intensified by a strong sense of former presence. Mould
began to grow over the deep wall by the window. There
were rustlings in the rafters above and she guessed something was nesting.

Her husband began to have bad nights. He said he didn't
like the moon rising into the roof light and filling it entirely,
so she cut up a makeshift curtain which she drew just
before getting into bed, but as he slept better she slept
badly, suffering from claustrophobia because she could no
longer see the stars.

Their long-suffering friend came and enthused over
everything and said,

'God, you're so *lucky* to have a place like this, a place in
Wales where you can get away from everything.'

He paced the width of the sitting room and said how
spacious it was and knocked his head on the beam which
ran across the centre, and set the spinning wheel turning
with the tip of his finger and said, 'Ah! The good life!
There's nothing like it,' and slept well despite the silence
which he didn't like to admit even to himself he found
rather frightening.

'Got a few potholes!' was the last thing they heard him
say as he bumped off down the drive, trailing his hand out
of the window like a tattered flag.

'*Dear Bernard*,' she thought, very glad he hadn't stayed.

'He's a pain in the arse,' her husband said, and slouched
off to his vigil by the waterfall.

Her spinning soon took over. The little scullery at the
back of the house was festooned with yarn dyeing and

drying, great hanks of it, brown and yellow and green and pink and purple. You could hardly move in there because of it. He told her the spinning thing was getting out of hand, but instead of being sorry, which a man might expect when his wife knows something she does affects him, she threw back her head and let out a peal of laughter. She was getting very jolly nowadays. He didn't like the way her neck arched when she threw back her head and he could see the smooth weals of tissue which made up the texture of her throat.

One day he caught her talking to a rough-looking man with two sheep dogs writhing at his heels. She was leaning over the gate talking to the man seemingly quite at ease despite the fact that the gate was wet and the rust was rubbing itself in big brown patches onto the clean fronts of her clothes. He hadn't got time for neighbours. Neighbours was one of the things he had wanted to get away from. He didn't go up to them but hovered in the background waving a bit of stick aimlessly and listening to the distant guttural sounds coming out of the man, he looked very rough and his hair was hanging down behind his ears, poking out under his cap in a grey frill. The man laughed once or twice, a short, whinnying sound. The woman looked over her shoulder but other than that gave no sign that she had noticed her husband. Later she said,

'That was our neighbour. Why didn't you come up?'

And getting no answer other than a grunt went on,

'He said his name's Hedd. I think it means "peace".'

And still getting nothing from him, settled herself at her spinning wheel and began deftly to draw out the thread.

She no longer thought very much about whether her husband was working. His unhappy face, with the lines of it all drawn downwards and his earlobes seeming almost to touch his shoulders, so much did he nowadays sink into himself, she saw as if entirely from outside, as though they were the dreary accoutrements of a stranger. She felt sorry for him and attended his needs quite assiduously, much as if she had been his nurse. She didn't like the way he watched her. It put her on edge. What she liked best was drawing out the thread, and planning in her head the patterns she would weave it into. First of all there would be a rug with triangles of red and blue, just a small rug, something quite small to begin with, because she had never woven anything before. Then a bigger rug, perhaps full room size, well, a small room anyway, creams and greens alternately, with unexpected jagged bits of saffron. And then there would be ... But the possibilities were almost endless, the permutations of colour and pattern dazzling in their variety.

In fact the first thing she made, because she had not yet got a loom, was a carefully crocheted belt. She had so much wanted to make something out of her beautiful skeins of wool, she couldn't wait for the loom, which she had chosen from a catalogue and ordered. So she crocheted a long belt (far too long, it would have gone round her own quite thin middle at least twice), using up all her colours and done in a tight mosaic pattern reminiscent of the headband she thought might have adorned the forehead of some ancient Inca deity. The result pleased her. She liked the way the colours fused when you looked at them quickly, as though a harmony had been achieved by her own chosen juxtapositions which was beyond anything she had hoped for. Her husband didn't like the very tight pattern. He said,

'My psychiatrist would have a ball with that one.'

But she refused to trouble herself with repression and envy and angst and dislocation, and delighted in the bright geometry her own hands had created.

She put a hook in the wall next to her spinning wheel and hung the belt there and admired it, sometimes consciously, sometimes in the back of her mind where it swayed as the winds of her imagination caught it up, like an enticing, multi-coloured flame.

The night by the fire, after the rain, when her husband had his very bad feeling (he was getting them frequently now, afraid of whatever lay outside the boundaries of himself, afraid too of what was within) and she suggested he should go up to bed, and he went, pressing his weight onto each of the wooden stair-treads so the whole thing seemed to shudder and she thought,

'Those stairs! Something will have to be done!'

– that night, after she had finished her spinning, at about eleven o'clock or perhaps it was half past, she sat quietly doing nothing for a few minutes and enjoying the bright belt hanging on its makeshift hook. She touched it once or twice and it felt good against her fingers. She thought, perhaps before the loom came she would make another. She liked making things. It quite surprised her.

When she had raked out the last of the fire and turned out the light, she went to bolt the back door, but opened it instead and stepped outside. It was very still. Even the waterfall seemed unusually subdued, and the smell of fresh things, some late buds and a flurry of young grass, sharpened up her nostrils and she lifted her head a little, like a dog sensing something coming from a long way off. It was also very dark indeed, a blackness filling the valley to the rim, and above the rim the sky invisible, not even the punctuation of a star.

She went in and shut the door and went upstairs with an uneasy feeling, but felt calmer when she saw her husband sleeping with his hand clenched against the side of his face, as a child sleeps.

She took off her clothes and folded them and got into bed with nothing on and lay against her husband's back and fell asleep herself quite soon. In the night he was very restless, much more restless than he had ever been. His restlessness woke her up, and it must have been five before she eventually went back to sleep, but even then uneasily, as if she was half aware that at any moment some random movement of her husband might disturb her again.

She didn't wake up until quite late, gone eight o'clock, feeling anxious, with that guilt and fear you tend to get when you are late, even though you may have nothing particular to do. Her husband was already up, which was unusual, a dent in the pillow where his head had been, and the sheets thrown back as though he had got out in a hurry. She lay on her back and listened, expecting to hear him moving about somewhere in the house. But it was quite quiet. The sun was just coming up over Craig y Ffynnon, the clear square of the roof light etching itself onto the farther wall.

She got out of bed hastily and pulled on some clothes. She didn't stop to do up her sandals, and they made a brash, slapping sound as she ran down the stairs.

'Ted!' she called. 'Ted?' and thought, where can he have got to?

She went into the sitting room and the first thing she saw was that her belt had gone. The empty hook looked startlingly solid, casting a short, blunt shadow on the wall. The woman swayed slightly, as you do when you begin to feel faint, everything recedes and you balance for that instant on the pinhead of existence. She thought, I ought to keep calm, and put her hand onto her ribs as though she could control her heartbeat by exerting pressure there.

She did up her sandals and walked quickly out into the yard and listened and then went across to the barn and pushed open the tall doors which swung apart with a creak. The interior was cavernous and placid. The great, dark rafters, punctuated by spots of light where the roof was going, were undisturbed. She said,

'God. *God.*'

Outside again she blinked and headed for the waterfall. Even before she got there she saw, or thought she saw, a flash of it, and a step or two later she did see it, her own precious belt, harmlessly adorning her husband's highish forehead as he sat on a rock by the stream with his dark red pencil in his hand and an exercise book poised industriously on his knee.

She said his name and he turned irritably towards her, but then smiled, a preoccupied kind of smile, and turned back to his work.

Later, back in the house and ticking things off on a list as she accomplished them, the woman's desire to strike her husband, the momentary overwhelming wish to see him dead, had almost entirely abated. She listened with tolerable composure as he went up the stairs, and when she heard the hard, two-finger rhythms of his typewriter begin, was nearly indifferent.

She didn't sit down to her spinning because the noise of the treadle and the wheel constantly turning was sure to disturb him. Towards the end of the afternoon she saw him going past the window with his hands in his pockets and his head held back at an angle. He looked as if he was whistling.

Later, much later, she went up to the bedroom and through into the little room tucked under the eaves and saw her belt hanging on the back of his chair. She picked it up and folded it into two and replaced it carefully. Then she tidied together the four typed sheets her husband had left spread out on his table and placed on top of them a fifth, blank but for the title typed in capitals, A PLACE IN WALES, and an inch or two below it, also in capitals, his name.

PUNISHMENT

•

Tessa Hadley

A woman who had arranged for the first time in fifteen
years of marriage an assignation with another man stared
into a glass case in the museum. Assignation. The word
was theatrical, ridiculous, like the whole business. Anne
could hardly believe she was there and dressed, she who
most mornings scarcely had time to notice what she dragged
on, dressed so agonizedly carefully for the part in her black
crêpe skirt and cream lace blouse. Cream lace for innocence, black for experience, she recognised, wincing.

In the glass case – when she focused – was a little sprawl
of bones. Not random, but laid against some kind of sandy
soil in the arrangement they had once been fastened in
with flesh. Human, child-sized, knees drawn up to chest.
Anne's eldest daughter always slept like that. The case had
been set up to look as though the bones – the same dusty
tan colour as the soil – had only just been uncovered, but
they had acquired irresistibly that museum-exhibit patina
of sad staleness, like the stuffed animals in the next room,
the baby otters in their frozen play, lustreless oyster catchers
by a plaster sea. It was hard to make oneself feel any sort of
connection with the bones, hard to care that they had ever
died. Anyway, Anne couldn't concentrate. Her excitement
– or dismay – was like swallowing iridescent bubbles of
oxygen which burst in her lungs and made consciousness
swim.

She had wandered at random into this exhibition of arte-
facts from a local Bronze Age site, she wasn't meeting him
here. But she was fifteen minutes early – good old Anne,
always so scrupulously punctual! – and she simply couldn't
have waited all that time in front of the painting she had
promised to show him. She hadn't even visited it yet, in
case it was bad luck, in case in her so-characteristic over-
punctiliousness she contaminated this chance too, this one
miracle of a chance.

She made herself read the printed information on the
boards behind the case. Oh: not a child, not male. So much
for her biology 'O' level. A woman in her twenties, dead –
and Anne was almost forty; but in those days of course
women were old by forty, worn out by child-bearing and
sickness and hard labour. There was no way of telling from
these bones if the woman had been beautiful – did that
matter? It hadn't mattered for years; for all these years
Anne had hardly looked in a mirror, or rather, she had
looked hastily in a mirror often enough, but only to check
she was presentable, that she could show herself at the
supermarket or the school playground or for one of Stevie's
appointments without her face betraying the chaos and
deep disastrous preoccupations of her daily life. That was
all she had looked for.

Liar, liar. She could see herself reflected in the glass side
of the case. Today it mattered. It was the only thing that
had ever mattered – and she had always known it, and all
those times she had glanced so contemptuously indiffer-
ently at herself she had done it lying, and out of spite and
vindictive rage, to make herself ugly in revenge for what
had happened to her, and today, when it mattered more
than anything, she would have to pay for her spite. At least
not fat: caring for Stevie and three healthy children at least

had that advantage. Too gaunt, probably. But even in the unsatisfactory reflection in the glass case – she shifted anxiously until the light was best, there was no one to catch her at it, the museum was so empty at that morning hour – she feared something wrong. Something gone from her face, squandered, forfeited in the dreary ages in that underworld of tiredness, month after month of night after night of three or four hours of broken sleep. Or was it just because while she wandered in that underworld the years of her life had passed on the surface without her noticing, and now she saw for the first time that she was almost forty? The natural blonde hair was turning a sad neutral colour on its way to grey. There were sharp-etched exclamation lines beside the corners of her mouth when she smiled – at herself, experimentally, in the glass.

Of course Gerry reassured her she was beautiful. But that didn't count: whatever he really saw, what else could he say? Kindness had been the basis of their life together for so long: how else could they have lived, under the circumstances? She had never told Gerry, for example, how she disliked the shiny bald patch like a secret duck pond in his hair. How funny, she had thought it a duck pond all these years and never even said it to herself. The duck pond with its fringe of greasy sparse hair he tried to brush across it. Or the pale pudgy flesh muffling his shoulder blades. Her dear, beloved Gerry.

But the man – the other man – must have liked her, to ask to meet her here. In ten minutes – still it wasn't time. He liked her: the way you know, even after all those years spent in the underworld. And perhaps, if you caught the reflection from a different angle, she wasn't so bad: in the well-cut camel-coloured wool coat she had bought in the sales this spring the week after the baby started school;

with her new haircut fastened with slides behind her ears, with ear-rings and perfume. Perhaps she looked interesting; perhaps she looked just the part for an assignation. Perhaps she looked as though she had suffered. And if he liked that – if she could transform it all into that, just for one moment (no, one hour, one hour) of his liking it – she would. She'd do anything.

Jesus, God. Seven minutes. But don't go to the picture yet. She strolled scrupulously from display to display around the rest of the Bronze Age exhibition. A curator hovered in the entrance from the main hall – perhaps he'd been suspicious of her long stillness in there. She studiously ignored him. That wasn't like Anne, who usually descended on these places queen bee to a swarm of noisy children, conspicuous with the wheelchair, mediating the intrusion she could not possibly contain with her brave, bright chatter, overcoming other people's awkwardness for them, making it possible for them to look at poor little twisted, gawping Stevie. 'He likes to come. He doesn't seem to see it but I know he likes it. The evening after we've been to something like this he's so calm. No convulsions.' It might be true. Sometimes she thought it was true. She knew Gerry didn't believe her but he didn't say.

She stared at brown pots the same colour as the earth and the bones, crazed with darker-coloured mends where they had been meticulously reconstructed out of fragments. A case full of weapons: as if there wasn't enough pain without them. A stone quern, displayed with a sheaf of barley or something like barley (hadn't she watched a video in here with the children once, about young archaeologists regrowing the original Bronze Age species?) and a handful of grains in its hollow. Thank God for sliced bread. Then a gold torque. For moments she thought it must be a reproduction, the gold softly shining like new, in contrast to everything else there in its colours and textures of decomposition, its process of returning to the colour and texture of the earth it came from.

Some lucky woman. It must have been heavy to wear – like a big collar, shoulder to shoulder on those child-sized people, little oblongs of gold linked together like chain mail – but who would complain? To be so singled out, so ornamented: Anne admired it with a little frisson of greed, she who had never bothered with jewellery in her life, didn't even wear a wedding ring because, caring for Stevie and the babies, she had to wash her hands so often it got clogged with soap.

Five minutes. On her way out of the room she paused at the bones again, read more from the printed board. The fractured skull – she hadn't even noticed. An execution. A sacrifice. Or a punishment for adultery. Well, there was nothing they could do to punish Anne. Times had changed. They couldn't knock her on the head with a stone, or take her children away, or her home, or lock her up in an insane asylum. And she didn't even care if Gerry found out, either. There was no punishment she was afraid of.

It seemed to have nothing to do with Gerry. She wasn't looking to replace him with a different husband, different marriage – God, no, fat chance of that anyway. With four kids? And one of them Stevie? She just wanted to be – lifted out, that was all. Just to be in a different life for an hour, an hour or so, out of that twilight of maternity she'd committed herself to in vengeful abandon, after Stevie, having the other two: Gerry hadn't wanted them, he'd known …

Perhaps it really scarcely mattered who. Of course she'd been thinking of him, imagining this *assignation*: all this past week, ever since the life-drawing class where she'd talked to him so entertainingly about the painting in the museum she'd loved when she was a little girl, and he'd said, 'Why don't you show me? Couldn't we meet there one day – for lunch, maybe?' The miracle, the miraculous chance: and how was it she had answered him so calmly, so maturely, as if she was the sort of woman who did this every day? 'But be prepared: it's awful. The painting: it's really the most treacly thing. And have you ever had lunch there? The café's actually called The Dinosaur. And I think it's what they put in the sandwiches.' She hadn't leaped at him. And he hadn't asked her with a leer. Serious. Shy, but not fumbling, either; she couldn't have managed it if everything about him hadn't been just right.

But when she imagined their meeting – dreamed of it: what else had she been doing, every conscious moment of this past week? – she didn't vividly imagine him, not his face, not his body, not even with any precision how much she liked him (because she had, from the first evening he joined the class; enormously). But – wasn't it funny? – what had turned her dizzy with excitement and fear every time she thought of it – knife poised over onion, chopping, or kneeling picking up bits of jigsaw from the floor, or doing Stevie's physio with Gerry – was the idea of a room, the room that he would take her to. He must have a room, mustn't he? A single man – separated. There must be somewhere they could go, and shut the door, and he would lay her on a bed with different sheets she'd never washed, and she could stare at unfamiliar pictures on the walls. Or better still, no pictures. And no sheets: bare mattress and white walls. Just a space with no messages: herself in it, and the unknown. The idea of that bare mattress – striped blue and cream ticking, and those little end tabs of cord that puckered it at intervals – had so excited her that a couple of nights ago she had surprised and gratified Gerry, nuzzling up to him amorously in bed. They didn't manage that kind of thing very often, under the circumstances.

There – it was time. She wasn't even early – he might be waiting for her. Now she hesitated: with a sudden tug of recognition she saw she was still standing by the little huddled skeleton, in Beth's sleep-time position, hugging her knees in her single bed, consoling herself. Poor old thing, thought Anne. When you need something desperately enough, not to get away with it – it's not fair.

Then another bubble of excitement. To reach the paintings she crossed the gallery above the end of the main hall, looking down over the handsome space, the splendid silvery glider suspended there ever since she could remember. The city's museum, founded on tobacco money, sugar money, slave money. Everywhere you went, you trod on bones. It couldn't be helped. She saw her painting from far off: he wasn't there yet. Bought like the bulk of the collection when the city's tobacco industry was still prosperous and bountiful, so that she'd grown up knowing her Holman Hunt and Burne-Jones better than Kandinsky or Picasso.

She knew every inch of this one, better than any other painting ever: wasn't that extraordinary? She had had it on a postcard beside her bed for years, she had made child-pilgrimages here. The lovers – illicit – meeting, separated by the railings: the little lace-gloved hand slipped through and held, her eyes cast down, his gazing meltingly, her costume of minutely painted satins and ruches and bows, pink and black, pink for tenderness, black for sorrow – damn! Anne recognised in horror: is that where I got it from? And hanging at her waist – so real Anne had once thought it a kind of magic – a little pair of ornate scissors, gold.

Anyway he was late. He had never meant what she had crazily fantasised. He would not come. Of course he wouldn't come – with a cold brusqueness she was sure – wasn't that just her life? And if he came shouldn't she pour out the truth at him. 'I'm an old woman, look, I've had four children, my breasts aren't what you're probably imagining …'

Then, as though the gallery settled into its empty peace around her, he was there. He walked towards her down the length of the blond wood floor, his footsteps shy and real, in the short dark leather jacket Gerry would never – could never – have worn. And she was happy. And as she remembered just how precisely he was everything she wanted, she also knew, with an anguish of vulnerability she hadn't felt for twenty years, just what her punishment would be.

KILLING THE HAY

•

Julie Rainsbury

It had been a year since Gwilym murdered his future once
and for all by killing the child. Now he watched the girl as
she paused at his gate, her face hate-twisted. She spat, as
she always did, across the white fence. The man with the
ponytail drew her away. Put his arm around her. They
thought he had done it on purpose, of course, out of some
kind of spite. It had been a deliberate act all right, he'd
admit that, but he had not known that the baby was there.
Dragged down by his own pride, his other neighbours
said. An old fool, showing off. Maybe. But what had he had
left except his past, his pride? He had murdered Nesta's
future too. Not that she said much. She did not pass judgement. She was a woman who understood pride but she
was pretty silent all round these days. Didn't go out like she
used to. They both kept themselves to themselves. Gwilym
watched the young couple walking on. Last year, at first,
things had not seemed so final. Gwilym cast his mind back.
Went over things again, over and over. Last year he had
watched that girl.

She passed along the lane, at the usual time, right in front
of his kitchen window. A gaggle of children followed her,
scuffling the dust, swishing their hands though long
grasses from the overhanging banks. Their voices were high
and clear in the afternoon air. The girl walked on, oblivious,

74

ahead of them. She carried her baby, cocooned in a canvas sling, pressed tight between her breasts. One brown arm cradled its bulk, the other wrapped a bunch of foxgloves, their shapes hazed in hot colour against the white-bright road. Gwilym lifted the curtain slightly, watched the pattern of crossed straps on her retreating back. She was whistling a tune, soft, between her teeth, her walk fluid to the tumble of notes.

'Dear God, they can't all be hers surely?'

His wife's voice made him jump.

'I think she just takes them to and fro to school, Nesta. Several of the people up there seem to have children. They say it's one of those communes now.'

He jerked his head, self-conscious in his interest, towards the hill.

'Hippies then. No telling with that lot.'

His wife gave a dismissive sniff.

'When I think how it used to be. You couldn't find a tidier place than Hendy. We had some times there. Old Mrs Evans must be spinning in her grave, poor soul.'

'Well,' Gwilym could hear the depression seeping back into his voice as he answered her, 'things change.'

Just thinking about it emphasised the stoop that was developing about his shoulders, seemed to make his very bones ache. Nesta sensed his altered mood at once.

'So did you ask them, then?' she queried briskly, turning away from him to twitch at boiling saucepans on the Rayburn.

'I saw Tom in the village. They won't be needing me this year. They've got the new machine, see. Set it against tax, he said. They're doing big bale. Big bale is all you hear these days.'

Gwilym grimaced with some bitterness.

'First it was the silage, now it's the hay. I can't afford to compete. Times are different and big machines cost big money. Lucky now we had no sons to follow on.'

He was ashamed of the last statement. His wife glanced at him. Resumed her stirring of pots.

'Well, you'd better get out back anyway and make sure that hitch on the trailer is fixed. Big bales also need big farms, remember. The smallholders will still be calling up as usual. There'll be a rush any day now, this weather.'

Gwilym shook his head.

'Dewi's not wanting to do his bottom fields because he's been told he'll get that grant for scientific interest if he lets them alone and Gelli Aur's sold theirs off as standing.'

He noticed the stern set of his wife's shoulders.

'But you're quite right, of course. It still needs doing.'

He edged hurriedly out of the door and crossed the yard towards the barn. Nesta was a good woman. She could live with failure, what she couldn't stand was self-pity. He knew that. He lifted his head to the distant hum of machinery. Watched for a moment the work progressing on the far hillside. The giant rolls of hay, black and slick in their plastic coverings, were already being fork-lifted and stacked at the field's edge. He turned his hands over and looked down at his palms, ran his thumbs on skin hardened by the cut of bailer twine. He lifted the latch on the barn door and went inside. He was in control in here. His tools hung, neat, along the wall. His machinery was cleaned, ready for the season. Out of date all of it now, of course, but still in good working order. Perfect, really, in its way. He lost himself for a while over the trailer hitch.

Later, when he returned to the kitchen, Nesta was bending to lift a steaming plate from the warming-oven.

'Where's yours then?' he asked as she set it in front of

his place beside a mug of tea and a leftover half of apple pie.

Nesta took off her apron and flicked a few crumbs from the ample front of her best blouse.

'I had mine earlier. I told you this morning. Choir practice. You know, with the Eisteddfod coming up.'

'Oh, yes.'

Gwilym cut into a potato, stirred it with the tip of his knife in a little of the rich gravy. The rush of summer choir practices were as perennial for her as the rush of haymaking used to be for him.

'I forgot, that's all.'

She kissed the top of his head. He felt the touch of her lips, light, through his thin hair. Gathering song sheets and handbag, Nesta clicked out of the door on her Sunday-chapel heels. The kitchen was quiet without her. She had shut the Rayburn down but it was still stuffy. Gwilym drank his tea and pushed aside the remains of apple pie. He wandered outside and round into the garden at the front of the house. He still felt uncomfortably warm. The evening was calm and he automatically checked the sky for signs of oncoming rain.

'Not that it matters much,' he muttered aloud to himself.

'I'm sorry?'

The girl was leaning across the fence towards him. He was startled by her sudden closeness.

'I'm sorry,' she repeated, 'I didn't catch what it was you said.'

'It doesn't matter.'

She opened the gate and came to stand beside him in the garden.

'I wanted to ask you something.'

'Yes?'

Her skin, in the V of her cotton top, was shadowed li

the bruise of thumb pressure on an apricot's flesh. Gwilym did not meet her eyes but tried to concentrate on a point somewhere around about her chin.

'We're cutting hay tomorrow and someone said you might be willing to come up and help us. We can't do it all by hand.'

'We don't cut hay around here.'

Gwilym was aware that surprise made his reply sound gruff – even surly. He looked up and saw that the girl was confused.

'We talk of cutting corn,' he explained, 'but in Welsh we call it killing the hay.'

'But you'll come,' she insisted, smiling now.

Gwilym looked again at the sky.

'How much are you doing?'

He cast a doubtful and experienced eye along the lane towards Hendy. Took in the tumble of corrugated iron and bracken-rusted fields that now formed its outlying boundaries.

'Only about twenty-six acres.'

He nodded thoughtfully. Those twenty-six acres would be the flatter, top land. Always had been the best.

'Tomorrow morning, then.'

Gwilym watched the girl until she was out of sight behind the far wall of the barn. A small smile played on his lips.

'Meinir said that girl from the hippies was down.' Nesta said to him as she climbed into bed that night.

Gwilym adjusted himself to the new slope of mattress

it.

much, Meinir.'

taking in the washing and her place
' Nesta excused the gossip. 'What was

'Contractor.'

Gwilym smiled again as he turned to sleep. The tautness that had been in his limbs for weeks relaxed. Tomorrow he must be out early on the hay. He snuggled, content, against his wife's back and thought of the fruit-fleshed girl.

Next morning, after the haze of dew had lifted from the grass, Gwilym hitched up his machinery and set off towards Hendy. He bumped down the rutted track to the farmyard which appeared as a vivid bustle of activity as the dust clouds settled about the tractor wheels. Young men and women, dressed in styles and colour combinations he had never contemplated, were busy about the yard. Children seemed to be everywhere. It was a relief to him when the girl came out to greet him. She wore a scarf, patterned blue, in her hair and carried the baby in her arms. Gwilym looked down and met its unwavering, wide-eyed gaze. He would have liked a son. Times were bad but children helped you to change. Made sure there was a future, even it if was different, difficult.

'We're going to cut the home meadow ourselves, by hand.' The girl indicated a field of about three acres just behind the cowshed. 'We like to use traditional methods if we can. Follow the old customs.'

Gwilym nodded dubiously. The girl seemed aware of his reservations. She flushed.

'We're not very experienced, of course, that's why we thought, you know, just this first year, that we'd better have you up to help with the rest.'

'Right, I'll get started. I know my way around the farm. If it stays fine, I'll be able to turn it as well late afternoon. You keep all those children out of the field though. I won't hear them from the tractor cab. It's dangerous.'

The girl noted Gwilym's rather curt tone. Struggling to make amends for whatever she had said wrong, she went on hurriedly,

'We'll be having lunch, a real hay-time picnic, in the home meadow. Come and join us when you've finished. We're trying to make it all just as it would have been in the past.'

Gwilym found himself unable to speak. It was his life, real work and sweat mind, that she was talking about. With a brief nod, he drove off through the gate into the first field. He worked methodically, as he always did, noting a lack of lime here, hedges in need of laying there, a farm on the brink of tipping into ruin. He tried to concentrate on the task in hand, not to let his memories of the place distress him.

At midday, he pulled the tractor back into the yard and walked uncertainly into the home meadow. Older children were carrying food, arranging it on a long table set in the shadow of twisted rowan and laburnum that crowded the hedge. The girl welcomed him with a smile, home-made beer. She handed her baby, in its wicker Moses basket, to two younger children with industrious rows of daisy chains threaded about their necks.

'Carry him around. He's worn out, needs to sleep.'

They set off, keeping to the hedgerow and swinging the basket gently between them. The other adults were working their way across the field. Armed with a motley assortment of old implements, an unlikely mixture of scythes and sickles, they made a jagged and uneven path towards the feast. Gwilym took a long swallow of the beer and laughed aloud.

'Does it bring back memories?'

The girl turned her face, damp, green in the tree-cool shade, towards him. Gwilym drank again. His eyes were distant. He no longer saw the ridiculous group before him in the field. He was young and green as sap himself: could feel the ache in the forward leg that took the strain of each smooth sweep of blade, felt old sun hot on the rhythm of his back, the fierce pride as he kept in line with the older men, matched their speed and skill, cut for cut. Other women were by the hedge, his mother, Mrs Evans, all the village and Nesta, thin as water, a handkerchief, blue-patterned, round her hair.

'More beer?'

Gwilym held out his glass to the man with the ponytail.

'Helena,' the ponytail bobbed towards the girl, 'was telling us what you said about killing the hay. Fascinating. It must be a really ancient phrase. All those bygone customs. Wonderful. You must tell us more.'

Gwilym looked at him slowly, surfacing.

'The hay, the corn, plenty of customs. A way of life.'

He paused and looked at the wreck of the half-cut meadow. Uneven, tufted, a waste. He suddenly felt an overwhelming anger. He caught up the sickle that the young man was holding. Strode out into the field. He called hoarsely over his shoulder,

'Here's another quaint one for you. At the corn harvest, the best reaper would cut the mare's tail, the final sheaf of corn. The year I married, I was the best. In the whole district, mind. The best.'

He glanced around. His eyes fixed on a particularly unkempt patch of hay that had been missed over towards the hedge. He wanted the girl to see what he had been. He braced his legs, felt strong in his skill, felt her presence behind him. He bent slightly and released the sickle in a smooth swished arc towards the stand of hay. The sun burned glorious on his back, flashed swift on the curving blade.

Back in the kitchen, Gwilym shuddered. He stood very still and seemed to listen to a sound inside his head. He had stood still a year ago in that field. He had been following the sure line of the blade with his eyes as the scream rose and hit the sky with a sudden chatter of birds. Gwilym had watched the girl. She flew past him towards the hedge, chased by two children trailing daisies. He remembered that her soft mouth had been skewed open, her face gaunt with fear.

HELSINKI MOUSE

•

Penny Windsor

It was her fourth cup of coffee and she had become familiar with the walk to the back of the large hall, down the steep stairs by the roulette tables, past the drunken man with the beard who tried to engage her in conversation by the empty cloakroom, and so to the tiny toilet cubicles. Each cubicle had a mirror and, reluctantly, she looked at her hair, untidy and unwashed from so many nights camping in the forest, and her swelling belly which she tried to hide beneath a large black T-shirt. If only her belly would just deflate as it had down over the years when she started her period, going down overnight like one of those party balloons which you find small and wrinkled the next morning. If only she could just breathe in, pretending that after all she had just put on a little bit of weight from eating all that heavy rye bread and cheese in the forest. But no, she ran her hand from her waist over her bellybutton to the curly black hairs between her thighs – it was taut and ripe, and showed absolutely no signs of being wished away.

She resumed her position by her empty coffee cup, sitting upright on the blue-grey sofa, as though any minute she would be off to catch a train. She didn't want to be mistaken for one of those non-travellers who had nowhere to go – the men full of lager who lived at the station, the bored young mothers with their toddlers, or the men who crowded two or three deep round the roulette tables. No, she was merely trying to make up her mind which train to catch. She had a purpose in being there – her indecision and excessive coffee-drinking due only to the fact that she was spoilt for choice. And, in order to make this clear to anyone who was watching, she cleared her throat, combed her hair and adjusted the straps of her rucksack. She had found a bright yellow plastic brooch on the seat, a child's brooch in the shape of a mouse, with large plastic whiskers and bright white eyes, and this she pinned to her shoulder bag. Maybe it would act as a talisman, bring her luck.

Actually she rather liked the station waiting room. It was warm and round, full of soft curves and lights, and should have been a good place to come to a decision. It wasn't like a British station at all, even the modern ones which served ground coffee. Dark-green stylish drapes were looped over the windows as one would expect in a theatre or a particular kind of café, a posh tearoom per-haps, the kind of place where people meet in plays and books, or going down-market, the drapes considerably dirtier, she imagined it as the kind of absinthe palace were Zola's characters became increasingly debauched. The tables had marble tops and low, shaded lamps, dividing the cafeteria from the restaurant area. Several large paintings dominated the wall, a lake with wooded islands painted in summer, and a few snowscapes. Besides the playing of machines and the hubbub around the roulette tables, there were occasional train announcements and distant music – Tom Jones, Frank Sinatra and Edith Piaf.

She watched the trees swaying in the wind beyond the drapes. They were in Helsinki – and the intermittent sun-shine and the storm clouds which came in from the harbour. But she was in a different self-contained world wrapped up in green drapes and soft lamps and snowscapes. Another

84

world, that is, until she had to make a decision and walk out of the heavy double doors beyond the roulette tables, going in one direction or another.

It had been his idea to come to Finland, a dream he had had for years from reading about the Finnish struggle for independence and the legends in their national epic, the *Kalevala*, through hearing the music of Sibelius and loving the forests. But she had been glad enough to come to this country with him. After all, she loved him, and they had agreed to share their adventures. But she hadn't foreseen the terrible row in the forest above the lake. And before that, she hadn't realised how vulnerable and tired the pregnancy would make her, so that in Helsinki, a city full of galleries and museums, elegant parks and sturdy monuments, she had felt herself floating into some sweet dream state in which history and culture passed her by, grand sailing ships whose construction and purpose were a mystery to her. And when he pressed her, told her stories, full of knowledge and enthusiasm, she began to feel she was playing some bit-part in Finnish culture – Lemminkäinen's mother in the *Kalevala*, for instance, after all his travels and adventures, putting him back together again, or Aino, Sibelius' pretty, shadowy wife who bore him six daughters. And then there were all those great stone statues of past men-presidents, whenever she walked in central Helsinki, and Mannerheim perched like a god on his horse outside the main post office. And inland, all the towns had names which sounded like semolina, and there was forest everywhere, sodden in the late summer rains and full of gnats ...

She knew she was being unfair – in fact she liked the forest, the mole which had burrowed around the edge of their tent each night, and the woodpecker hammering each morning at the high branches – and the lake with the jetty where she could swim into the far deserted centre and watch her swollen breasts and belly floating as though they were no part of her. And the Finns seemed a decent enough people, courteous, reserved, they liked trees, kept their toilets clean ...

But how could she come to any decision about her life if she was always so reasonable? If she could only indulge in some bitterness, self-pity, prejudice, she would be well on the way to walking out of the station waiting room in one direction or another. All this sweet reason and appreciation and seeing everyone's point of view was getting her no-where.

He turned over in the small tent feeling the space where he had so often stroked her breasts, which were now so big and tender, and the rise and slope of her belly, tight as a drum. The birch trees spattered the roof of the tent with raindrops and another shower, coming in from the lake, emptied out of the grey patch of sky beyond the mosquito net.

He loved her, he had told her. It was *her* body, he had told her. She should choose.

Then why was she so unreasonable? Why did she talk so obsessively about giving birth to a dead child, to a child with no head or limbs? Why did she rave so, that she wanted her body back as though it had been stolen from her? As though he had taken part in some plot to steal her body, her future, her freedom?

After all these days in the forests he had read and dreamed about, all these sweet, rain-filled days, the wild wind-blown lake at Karelia and here in the forests sur-rounding Hämeenlinna, home of Sibelius – she had turned on him, dangerously fierce, like some starved caged dog, and yelled at him for his reason, his patience, his understanding. 'You can only ever be a man,' she had yelled in that terrifying, high-pitched voice of hers, 'you think like a man and feel like a man – between your ears and between your legs'.

He could not answer. She had made him feel like the character Kullervo in the *Kalevala*, the narrow-minded inflexible one, bound by a single purpose and by duty, when during all his growing-up years he had identified with Lemminkäinen, the reckless adventurer who loved life, enhanced life for other people. Now he could only feel the child growing inside her and wonder. It was to be her decision. But he would not stretch out into the space that had been her space. He lay in the forest of his childhood dreams, and waited.

Child of mine, shall I let you live? Shall I witch you into life so you have no choice but birth, survival? Toss you into a rotten, beautiful world and see what you make of it? And I, your mother, what kind of mother is that, who already does not know whether she wants you, judges your life or death, carries you around waiting for a day of sunshine, a story, a man, to decide your fate?

You could die even now, quite easily, miscarried understandably from this forty-year-old body, swimming and running, walking rough forest tracks, sleeping on ground ridged with roots, pitted with stones and weeds. You have several ways of dying already, though you have even now missed the gentle scraping away of the contents of the womb, it being too late for that. But there are the twelve- or eighteen-week labour pains which will throw you out on some hospital bed, a non-child, a child who might have been, a bunch of cells, nothing much. Or you can grow, be allowed to grow, inside the body which is not sure it wants you, – but be mindful you have all your limbs and senses about you. Less than normal, too many imperfections, and you will be left this time alive, to be taken off by strangers. On this, he and she, she and he have agreed. Their lives cannot stand too much disruption, their freedom cannot be too drastically curtailed.

Or perhaps your best plan would be to escape like the legendary Aino captured by the old magician, Väinämöinen, just pretend to die, and while no one is watching, change quickly, becoming a creature of the lake and swim away into the very centre where no one ever goes and no one will find you.

So, child of mine, having come this far, come to the forests of Karelia and Aulanko, you wait in the waiting room of Helsinki railway station behind dark-green drapes, for a decision to be made.

She wished she was like some of those strong women characters she had read about in the *Kalevala*. Louhi, for instance, the witch who changed herself into a bird and attacked the men who had dared to take away the 'sampo', her treasure, her daughter's dowry. Louhi wouldn't be sitting on Helsinki station, brooding, introverted, thinking in circles. She would have done something positive, acted. But she obviously lacked that quality the Finns called 'sisu' – youthfulness, independence of thought, guts – or something like that. Instead she could see herself, a small, dark Western European woman in her fortieth year unable to make her mind up over what was, after all, a very commonplace dilemma. In the scale of things – Finland's fight against the Soviet Union for instance, or Lemminkäinen's deadly fight with the giant swan, it almost vanished as anything but the tiniest personal problem in an unimportant life.

After all it was simply a matter of making up her mind. Her doctor was modern and young and had outlined all her options – the tests she could have, the chances of abnormality, the ease with which she could have an abortion – immediately – because of her age, if this is what she wanted.

She had seen the time in Finland as a time to think away from home, the familiar, but not on Helsinki station. There were really only three options, all beyond those double doors. She could go back to Hämeenlinna and the tent in the forest. She could go to Helsinki airport and catch the plane home, or she could catch the train across the Russian border to see Leningrad, the adventure he and she had planned together. She could see now that once she had made the decision about where she was going from the station waiting room, the rest would be simple.

The clouds still hung low over the lake in the Aulanko forest, and the rain dripped through the birch trees. The mole burrowed busily among the sodden leaves and twigs now that the tent had gone.

Her doctor put away the last patient's notes and returned to her own children, to pack for their annual holiday in Greece.

A seagull dozed on Mannerheim's head.

She looked at the yellow plastic mouse with the bright eyes and smiled for the first time since she had left the forest. 'Let the mouse decide' she said, and pushing her coffee cup to the far edge of the marble-topped table, she walked confidently through the double doors, in one direction the other.

89

THE WIN

•

Alex Ward

They were the poor whites of the mountain bus, waiting by their farm gate. The two boys in ancient hand-me-downs of worn uniform grey; the two girls in washed-out summer dresses with let-down hems, and old brown sandals, summer and winter. Thin, pale and close together, defensive. They looked neither to right nor left, but took their customary seats, half-way between the smokers at the back and the modest first-years at the front, and spent the rest of the journey staring expressionless out of the window. They never indulged in the banter provoked by each newcomer hauled up into the steamy, noisy, smelly mayhem that lurched from stop to stop. The Tanners, like sick animals, did not run with the herd. Satchels and cigarettes flew over their heads. They neither ducked nor flinched. They were not even worth baiting. It was as if they did not exist at all.

Like most of the mountain kids they lived on a farm hidden from the road up a dirt track, but unlike their fellows they were never visited nor did they visit the other farms. It was rumoured that their dada had chased their mam with a meat cleaver all over the mountain. That was about ; about them, but since it was not)ccurrence in some form or another : notoriety soon wore off. Until, that pers; not for murder, as you might ise of a substantial pools win, several ine in those days.

The school bus stopped at their gate as usual, and for once everyone was looking out for them, all crammed to one side like passengers flying over the Grand Canyon, but they did not appear.

The next thing anyone knew was that the Tanners were selling up and moving into town to a house with a bathroom, a scullery and a fire with a back boiler. Before they left the mountain, they did the rounds of visiting their neighbours on all sides. To say goodbye, they said, but it was more in the way of a victory roll. Whatever the case, they caused a stir wherever they went. Nobody on the mountain was rich – the Tanners had acquired, along with the money, a certain glamour. The best tea cups, if such existed, were brought out, cakes and tinned peaches provided, and proper tablecloths smelling of mothballs. They were fêted and held sway in front kitchens all over the mountain.

Initially, the girls were timid and stayed close to their mam as she described in detail the new house, and their futures. But although they never left her side they were beginning to show signs of smugness and pride, as they made a great show of smoothing down the skirts of their new brightly patterned dresses, tugging their pink angora boleros and pulling up their dazzlingly white cotton socks, or flicking invisible motes of dust off their glossy black patent shoes. The boys, too, seemed visibly to expand, especially the eldest, Dafydd.

'You can have anything you want,' his dada said smiling hugely at the expansive freedom his sudden wealth allowed. And Dafydd knew right away what he wanted. Something that would change him forever, forever wipe away the image of his present self, and he knew where to find it. He saw it every day as he passed the gentlemen's outfitters at dinner time. The sports jackets were grouped together on the right of the window, set apart from the dull grey suits, pinstripes and funeral overcoats. Dafydd saw the group as young men, dashing, worldly-wise, adventurous and brave, everything he aspired to be. The hero stood just in front of his fellows, a natural leader – the dark navy blazer with shiny brass buttons embossed with anchors, a glittering badge of golden thread, fabulous beasts and mysterious writing. He would have that blazer, be that man.

By the time they got round to visiting Pen-y-wern, the girls were as cute and fluffy as calendar kittens, and the boys as plumped up and self-satisfied as pet runts. Their mam had their respective futures rehearsed in every detail. Mr Tanner would go into business in a small but successful way, as soon as he could settle on one amongst the many options now being offered him. The girls would marry small busi-nessmen and have touring holidays in Devon and Corn-wall. The boys would go into their father's business. It was all settled.

Dafydd had heard every performance of their projected future, but was growing weary at its postponed com-mencement. His dada's enthusiasms changed almost daily. Dafydd wanted his new life to begin at once. He wanted to be able to say 'I work in my dada's shop … garage … café …', and to choose the paint, put up the sign 'Tanner and Sons', so that everyone would recognise him as a figure of some standing in the community.

His mam was about to tell the story of the arrival of the pools win letter for the nth time. Dafydd went to look for Carys. He used to see her every day on the school bus, but had never addressed a single word to her or given her any sign that he was aware of her. Yet, if forced to do so, he could have detailed every aspect of her physical form – her yellow hair plaited like harvest bread; her calf-brown eyes and wet black lashes; the way the sunlight illumined the soft fair down on her arms like a visible aura; the dark mole on her upper lip; the tender column of her neck emerging from the crisp white collar of her school blouse; the tantalising glimpses of her lean tanned legs below the sharp pleats of her spot- and speck-free navy gymslip. His heart fluttered and thudded with excitement at the thought of coming upon this object of his desire.

The day was hot and grey. Small flies crawled feverishly amongst the sour cream flowerets of the elders overhanging the steep yard. Dafydd's new shoes pinched his toes and rubbed his heels. His grey flannel trousers felt as if they were made of thick felt. The blazer hung heavy like armour on his shoulders, but he would not be parted from it. He felt like some ancient dispossessed prince returning to claim his lost princedom, full of energy, excitement, anticipation. And then, there she was, sitting on the gate under the whispering beech trees, the low-backed bracken-covered hills lying like huge animals beyond the farm fields behind her. He felt his heart stop, but it resumed its frantic clamour concealed beneath the splendour of his navy serge. Like an automaton, his feet propelled him on towards the desired and feared encounter, and, suddenly, he knew it would be all right. He would not break down. He was different, wasn't he? When she looked at him she would see what he had seen when he looked in his mother's wardrobe mirror that morning – the leader of the pack.

She got down when she saw him coming. She was wearing a stripy t-shirt and grey pleated skirt. He had never seen her out of uniform before. He thought she looked like a film star – beautiful, casual. He wanted more than anything now to see her recognition of him, his new resplendent self.

But she made as if to walk past him without acknowledgement of any kind, as if nothing had changed, wilfully ignoring him. Once he would have stood back, defeated, but for the first time in his life he felt he could do something, make things happen. He blocked her way.

'What you doing then?' he said, waiting, willing her to look up at him.

But she didn't, wouldn't. 'I gorra do the chickens,' she said, side-stepping him and sauntering on down the yard to the 'next place'. He followed her, keeping close as she lifted the worm-eaten lids of the corn bins and scooped out the pellets and corn. When she climbed the stile to the back field, he climbed it too, and watched her as she stood with her back to him throwing the corn in an arc up into the hot grey sky, pelting the nettles in a desultory sort of way.

'What you doing now?' he said, drawing closer, gaining strength of purpose from the knowledge that she could not easily shake him off, and would have to acknowledge him presently however much she might resist.

'Nothing.' She picked up a stone and threw it at a clump of rushes, hitting it. He followed suit, but already she was walking off while he was still aiming, and did not see him score.

He followed her into the cool damp milky gloom of the dairy. The wet slate slabs smelt of milk. She took up one of the brass-handled measures, dipped it into a churn and drank from the measure, tipping it up until the milk ran in creamy rivulets down her small pointed chin, slender neck and down into the t-shirt. He stood in the doorway watching, totally absorbed, his imagination following the trickling liquid, indulging in his freedom to look at her. Finished, she hooked the measure inside the lip of the churn and turned to leave, but seeing she could not easily pass without touching him, she hesitated, waiting. He made no move to let her by. He had never felt so powerful before. He would force her to look at him, properly, see him for what he now was. When he did not move aside, her impassivity and indifference altered imperceptibly, as the silence, like the small physical space between them, took on a new significance, gave a meaning which she had studiously been avoiding to the encounter.

He waited, at ease with himself, in control. And then, as he knew she would, she looked directly at him, examining him, his shoes, his flannels, his blazer, taking it all in, assessing what she saw: the brass buttons, the baroque gold embroidery of the badge with its carefully stitched Latin tag. He still said nothing, waiting, confident, watching her still, small face. Then, pointing at the badge, she said, 'What's it mean?'

'Mean?' He was thrown off guard, floundering.

'Yes, mean?' she repeated, and he felt her finger strike the magic mysterious words beneath the fabulous crest, felt the heat start all over his body, rise humiliatingly to his face; the sweat like water pooling in his fists, staining his shirt, penetrating the thick cloth under his arms. He felt he could smell the humiliation, that she could smell it.

'I gorra go now, see,' he mumbled, letting her pass.

Years later he saw the Latin tag again, carved over the doorway of a school where he'd gone for a caretaker's job he didn't get. There it was, the same magic incantation, *Scientia est potentia*. But this time, like a distorted mirror image of itself, its English translation was carved alongside. '*Scientia est potentia*', he whispered to himself, '*Scientia est potentia*. Knowledge is power.'

A VERY PRIVATE AFFAIR

•

Christine Harrison

They weren't used to seeing babies in the nuthouse, she thought. Babies didn't go nuts. Only their mothers.

The nurses had loved him. Fussing round, all wanting to change his nappy. Made a nice break from the usual routine. They circled round the laughing, kicking little thing like broody mares round a new-born foal. They creamed him, dusted him with powder, held his little flailing feet in their hands.

'Stephen,' they sang and cooed to him. 'Stephen.'

The patients could go hang for a little while, moodily leaning round the edges of the room, tapping their fingers, biting their nails, rubbing their foreheads. No one was taking any notice of them.

And she had lain on her bed and watched. The nurses playing with her baby. The other patients waiting for their tranquillizers. It was all better forgotten. You should live in the present, that's what you should really do.

Which was this. The nativity play in the nursery school. Watching Ivy in her nativity play. Ivy had the plum part – she was the Virgin Mary.

Mothers and fathers, brothers and sisters sitting on low ⟨...⟩r the play to begin. But it had already ⟨...⟩hearsed impromptu entertainment by a ⟨...⟩m.

⟨...⟩' said the teacher, 'and be quiet.'

Then stiff-looking shepherds, like cut-out cardboard fig-
ures, shifted on to the stage, surrounded and outwitted by
drunken-looking, crazy, skittish sheep kicking their back
legs and generally over-acting. These were followed close
behind by the three kings, heads piled high with exotic
pineapple crowns or jewelled turbans. Ivy was looking for
her Mummy in the audience.

She gave Ivy a very small wave and thought how hard
she found it to live in this 'should be happy' present. Something pulling her back, always pulling her back. Pulling so
strongly.

Waiting for their tranquillizers, she thought, it was all
they ever did. It was a waiting game, alright. One of the
patients, a tall lovely woman with long dark hair had begun
banging the windowsill with a spoon.

'Just coming, Deirdre. Hang in there Deirdre. Just let me
put the nappy pin in. Never put on a towelling nappy before.
There's an art to it. The paper ones are easier.'

'They're wasteful,' said another nurse, 'expensive.'

'It's time for my tablet,' shouted Deirdre between clenched
teeth.

'Not yet dear. Two o'clock. Look at his dimply legs, Sister.
How much do you think he weighs?'

'I'll get the scales.'

'Oh yes. The scales. Get the scales. Have we got some
scales?' One of them ran off to find some scales.

But it was now that should matter. It was this. It was Ivy
dressed in the blue dress she had found in the Oxfam with
a white veil over her hair. Ivy with glasses because of a
slight squint. Just right for Mary, the glasses especially,
holding the doll with one ear chipped off, in a very still and
holy way that was enough to bring tears. Joseph was trying
to get the sheep in order but it was no use.

'Give me that crook, Oscar,' said the teacher, taking it away just in time.

She smiled at this. It was as if she were two people. While one smiled at Oscar's antics and at her daughter's portrayal of the Queen of Heaven, the Mother of God, another looked back with a blanched bleak look to that earlier scene.

'He's lovely. He's a lovely boy.'

Eager hands had begun divesting the little boy of his woolly jacket and socks, his stretchy playsuit and vest.

He shrieked happily. They took his nappy off again to weigh him. One of the nurses had come over to her.

'You've got a lovely little boy there, Margaret.' She looked reproachful. She meant fancy going off your rocker when you should be looking after him.

It had happened a long time ago. Time does not really pass at all. Time even reiterates and strengthens some things. Time – what is it anyway?

She was singing 'Away in a Manger' with the rest. It was not her favourite carol. But she sang in a humming sort of way. Sometimes she stopped singing and listened to the others; one of the mothers had a pleasant contralto, but most of them could not sing and the children sounded like a nest of birds, high and twittering.

Then it was time to go home for tea. Mum and Dad and little daughter with her specs and her warm navy hat with red bobbles, gloves to match, a proper little family.

'What's for tea, Mummy? I'm hungry.'

'We're all hungry. What's for tea, Mum?' said her husband. Her husband was Peter, thin, tall, blue eyes, a bit anxious-looking.

'Fish,' she said.

'Horrible,' said Ivy, her specs glinting, her holy look quite gone.

'Nice,' said Peter.

A proper little family.

Only something lay over them like a miasma. Only there was something, an unspoken, half-buried something that lay between them and around them, like a cold, half-imagined miasma.

Though it had started out well, as if it was going to be all right.

Margaret, spinster of this parish, and Peter had a very quiet church wedding. Just the two of them and a couple of witnesses. No church bells. No music. No confetti. Just the fallen cherry blossom blowing across the church path in the keen little wind. And then they had gone to the Italian and had pasta and a bottle of good red wine. Then back to the flat and so to bed for the afternoon. It had been a lovely wedding.

A year or so later Ivy had been born. 'You can't call her that dreadful name!' said everyone. 'We like it, it's a lovely name,' said Margaret. 'I love it,' said Peter. 'Ivy Isherwood – it sounds really posh, she'll love that name.'

And all the time it was as if they were walking in a fog, hoping that somehow, all at once, it would disperse. Of course she knew what it was about, she was not without insight. She knew, and so did Peter, that it was about Stephen, and about her half-smothered feelings for her first-born child. It was one thing knowing.

She simply could not talk about it to anyone. She had been, as it were, struck dumb. Tongue-tied. Speechless. Perhaps there were no words. It was as if part of her were paralysed.

Peter knew the facts. She had had a child at seventeen. She had been very ill after the birth. Having no support or family, she had been persuaded to give the child for adoption. He knew the facts – that was all. She might have gone through the motions of her life thus. Only something intervened on the Sunday before Christmas when they lost Ivy at the Home for Gentlefolk, as Peter called it.

They went there once a fortnight to visit Peter's mother. The place was decorated for Christmas; over-decorated, you could say. It was quite hard to find the old people among the mass of paper chains and glittery garlands.

'Mrs Isherwood is underneath the Christmas tree,' said the matron. What on earth could she mean?

'At least she's not on top of it,' said Peter. 'Ah, here she is. Hallo, Mother.'

The old lady was sitting in a ring with several other gentlefolk around the most tremendous Christmas tree. It smelled deeply of its piney needles and sappy resinous branches. Each of the gentlefolk had a box of decorations and was waiting for the word to start decorating with Matron's help. Mrs Isherwood had a box of stars.

'I want them all to go on top of the tree,' she said to Peter. 'Right at the top, they would look silly on the bottom branches.'

'Perhaps Ivy could help you,' said Margaret.

'I don't want Ivy to help,' said Mrs Isherwood, 'and anyway she can't reach.'

Ivy was allowed to hand things to Matron and they spent the afternoon making the tree beautiful.

Then they all sat round and admired it and drank cups of tea and ate custard cream biscuits.

'Oh it's beautiful,' everyone said, 'better than last year.' Margaret collected the cups and took them out to the kitchen. A ginger cat slept there in its basket in the warmth from the double Aga. Margaret had expected Ivy, whom she had not seen for a little while, to be in there – she loved the cat and usually came and talked to it on these visits.

'Where's Ivy?' she asked Peter. They both started looking everywhere. In the television lounge, the conservatory.

'I'll look in the grounds,' said Peter.

'I'll look upstairs,' she said.

Matron looked uneasy. 'The residents don't like to be disturbed,' she said.

She rudely ignored this and began leaping up the staircase two steps at a time. She was full of fear. It was silly, she knew that, knew she was overreacting. She always did when it came to this sort of thing. She imagined Ivy's throat cut by a deranged old person. She imagined, her heart like a stone, that she would never see Ivy again. That she would never be found.

She began opening bedroom doors, Matron panting behind her.

'Ivy,' called Margaret, 'Ivy, where are you?'

Then, 'Oh Ivy! What are you doing?'

Ivy was sitting on a chair by an old woman's bedside. The old woman lay in the bed with a white bedspread, her old hands like dried leaves with all the veins standing out, her mouth opened slightly. Beside her in the bed, tucked in with her, was a doll.

'She wanted my doll,' said Ivy. 'To hold.'

Matron and Peter stood in the doorway. They were very still. The old woman was very still indeed.

At last Matron went forward and felt the old lady's pulse. She shook her head. 'She's gone,' she said quietly. Gently she took the doll away out of the bed and gave it back to Ivy.

On the way home in the car, Peter said,

'Strange how she seemed to want something to look after – even at the end – the old lady, I mean.'

Ivy sat in the back of the car, the doll tucked into her safety belt on her lap. She had put a bonnet on to cover up the chipped ear.

'Did the old lady die?' she asked.

'Yes,' said Margaret, 'she was very old and tired and she died.'

'I know,' said Ivy.

Margaret herself had been deeply interested by the sight of the old woman. So old. So very old that the flesh had almost dried up on the bones, the skeleton showing, as it were, through hand and cheekbone and jaw. Her old face wrinkled by her long life, next to the smooth pearly pink face of the doll. Both had their eyes closed, the old woman's for ever.

Later that day Peter said, 'I felt what happened was good for Ivy. She just absorbed what happened in a natural way.'

Margaret felt the weight and texture of her husband's response to the incident. She knew him to be humane and perceptive. But there was something about it all she had to fend off.

'Better than having your guinea-pig die?' She was speaking in a callous, tasteless way. Why did she step back, cover things up, try to be clever?

Peter did not reply to this.

'It was a smashing Christmas tree,' was all he said.

That night she dreamt, as she often dreamt, of Stephen. He had just been born in her dream. And the old lady in the nursing home was a sort of midwife. An old crone of a midwife with almost a touch of the witch doctor about her. Although she was very old she could move very fast and was whirling round and round the room with the new-born baby in her arms.

'It's safe with me,' she kept saying. 'It's safe with me.'

'But I want him back,' said Margaret in her dream, and in her dream she felt a deep longing to have her baby back in her own arms. But the midwife crone disappeared out of the door, still saying, 'It's safe with me.' And Margaret woke up, the tears running down her face. Peter was already awake, propped on one elbow. He was watching her.

'You were talking in your sleep,' he said. 'You're crying.'

'What was I saying?'

'You were saying, "Help me".'

'Help me?'

'Yes. That's what I want to do.'

There was a long silence between them, Peter still propped on one elbow, staring at her steadfastly in the half-dark of the approaching dawn.

'Tell me about the dream.'

'Forgotten it.'

'Remember.'

'I can't.'

'Yes. Yes. It was about Stephen, wasn't it?'

'It was about the old lady who died.'

'And Stephen.'

'Yes, I suppose so. There was a baby in the dream. Yes. Yes.'

She started to cry properly, to sob. And then it was as if something broke, like a membrane breaking. And it all poured out. Suddenly. All her grief poured and flooded from her. It would not stop. It gushed from her as from a mortal wound. She rocked and cried out and shuddered and moaned.

Peter got out of bed and closed the door so as not to wake Ivy, then he held her as one might someone who is about to drown. 'Poor Mags,' he kept saying. But there was relief in his voice, a kind of glorious relief, as when it rains in a desert.

CLOUDED GEM

•

Kusha Petts

Edie smelt. Smelt of fish and chips. The heavy odour of frying oil clung to her clothes and seeped into every pore of her skin. When didn't it? Sundays and the Mondays they didn't open. Even then the smell was still in her nostrils. At first she had thought she would never stand it; now she was used to it – well, almost – and was, in any case, well-practised in quoting: 'needs must when the Devil drives' – the Devil being the necessity of earning a living.

They'd been late finishing up tonight. Still, the takings were good and that was what was needed. Moving about her own kitchen now, she yawned and repeatedly shifted her weight onto her right leg; the veins in her left calf were aching again. 'Course they are, she thought. Been on me feet too long. No help for that. You can't run a business sitting on yer backside.

Frank was already in bed. She could hear him turn over heavily in the room above. She thought: sure as eggs he'll soon be shouting down. He never could bear her to be downstairs by herself, though why he couldn't be content to drop off she couldn't fathom. After all, he slept the sleep of the dead, once he was away.

She heard Frank thumping the bedside table.

'Eed,' he called thickly, 'Eed-ee, wha' you doin'? An't you ever coming up? Wha' you doin', Eed?'

She gave no explanation, just answered from the kitchen door, 'Shan't be long. Shan't be two ticks.'

She smiled to herself as she imagined his reaction if she'd said exactly what she was doing at so late an hour, since, for no reason that she gave to herself, she had no intention of going to bed until she had cleaned her rings. It might be stupid at midnight but she wanted them sparkling again: her engagement ring, three graduated diamonds of modest size and quality, and the 'dress' ring that had been her mother's, a half-hoop of sapphires set with diamond chips. Maybe she was silly to wear them for work in a fish and chip shop, she reflected, but she didn't feel right without them. All evening, in the pressure of frying, serving and deftly wrapping steaming parcels, the rings had kept catching her eye. They were not just temporarily clouded in the atmosphere; they really needed a proper clean as well.

Her middle-aged fingers had coarsened and now she had to soap her knuckles to ease the rings from her fingers. She set the last of old Granny Watkins' china egg cups on the kitchen table, put in the rings and poured over them some methylated spirits, just as she had seen her mother do many times when she was a child.

'God A'mighty,' she said to herself, 'I used to eat me eggs outa that egg cup when I was a nipper.' She had a brief vision of her pig-tailed self in the far world of childhood, cracking a Saturday teatime egg and burning her fingers flaking off the top bits of shell. Kids. Well, she'd seen her own three girls grow up. Sound and healthy. Doing alright. And here was Marie, her 'baby', about to have her own first. In less than three months.

Marie. How on earth was she going to manage without Marie? A good quick worker and no messing. But her Geoff was already on at her to give up right now. And you couldn't blame a son-in-law like him for not wanting his wife all hours in the fish and chip trade and coming home smelling of it. Edie was resigned to the job. But why should Marie be, if she didn't have to? She and Geoff could get by and Geoff was a smart one with his extra bodging, making a bit of the old ready on the side. Good luck to them. Especially now they'd found a little flat and weren't squeezed in with her and Frank any more.

Edie stirred her rings gently with her forefinger and sighed. Oh, how she'd miss Marie. Not just in the work, but as company. Always good for a little laugh, was Marie, even when things were dodgy. And Frank would never do the extra work. Not that he couldn't. Just wouldn't shift himself. And too fond of nipping across to the Falcon. Plain lazy where any real issues were concerned. In small ways too. Like that stinking mushy spud she'd found skidded underneath the chipper, smelling to high heaven. He'd dropped it. Too damn lazy to bend. Yeah, he said, knew it was somewhere. She shuddered, remembering her revulsion as her fingers sank into the putrid substance. Lazy sod.

Should she try for a man or a woman to replace Marie? Full or part time? She would have to sort it out. And soon. Marie was getting too bulky and too tired. Edie bustled about and set breakfast while her rings were soaking. Tomorrow was another day already knocking on the door. She placed freshly laundered overalls on a chair back; you had to look spick and span in this business, start off the day right, no matter what.

'Eed,' shouted Frank in a tone at once petulant and commanding. 'Oh, bugger the man!' said Edie out loud, but quickly finished cleaning the rings, gently brushing the stones with a soft old toothbrush. When Frank shouted again, a long-drawn-out 'Eed,' she went quietly upstairs, automatically avoiding the squeaky board on the top step.

In a warm but unbecoming flannelette nightdress she stood by the window, the March moon just on the wane. She slipped the dress ring into its original little box, very aware of her mother's worn fingers occasionally handling it. The box was once deep red, a red now faded and patchy at the corners, but real leather and well-made with its fine little brass clasp. Why bother, she mused? Yet it gave her a distinct pleasure to bed the ring in the discoloured satin slot. The sapphires glowed richly. As if they had a life she wanted to keep close, she put them not on the dressing table but on the small table on her side of the bed.

A late car drew up a few doors down. Huw Johnson again, the stop-out. Never with his wife. Suddenly the quiet of the night was pierced by the howls of a cat. The Jenkins' Tom Moggy, on the rampage.

'Damn noise,' grumbled Frank, his voice slurred with sleepiness and irritation. 'Damn bloody ca's. Chuck a boot at 'em.' Edie looked out of the window and saw the flash of a black and white cat with a big tabby in pursuit. As she watched the chase, to her astonishment her mind was flooded with a small incident in her youth, a day during the war, in the year in which she met Frank. She was still new to being with him, still new to what had been the wonder of physical love. Frank. Tall. Slightly fleshy. Good-humoured, with a slow sort of charm and lazy-lidded blue eyes. She liked his voice with its soft Welsh accent, so different from the nasal twang of the London suburbs she knew. His voice was unremarkable to her now and his body, thickened and paunchy, spelt plain indolence.

He was an acceptable and cheery cove in the Falcon bar, alright, and as long as nothing came to cross him, pleasant enough to customers when in a good mood. But long ago she had agreed with herself; he was essentially an idler, a burden on her back, to be humped as best she could. After the Army life he had never had any clear ambition or particular skills to offer and his self-indulgence and lack of 'go' had cost him many a job. The fish and chip venture was a last resort, and it was paying off, getting them clear of debts at last. Steady trade. And as much as could be handled on mart days. Coming back to Frank's home town, his old stamping ground would – she hoped – shame him into putting a better face on things, pulling his weight more. That hope went west; he was only quick enough to seek out former drinking cronies. Edie had to be the main drive, the organizer, the one who kept things under control; but since it was all working out she was grateful enough.

Now, standing in the window, she lost all sense of time, felt transported back to a little house in a side-street in Salisbury where Frank had found her lodgings so that they could meet in his off-duty hours from the camp at Bulford. She had filled in the time with barely-suppressed excitement, waiting for the evenings. Waiting for him. Dear God. Waiting for him … Her landlady, Mrs Butler, bustling with kindness and gossip, was utterly haphazard and muddled in her habits; never one to wear out a broom or duster. Edie recalled the back scullery: two steps down into an ill-lit, cluttered place where she had offered to wash up, feeling that a bit of her private scouring of plates and pans would at least make the rough meals a little more hygienic and therefore a little more palatable. Drying a chipped blue enamel saucepan one day, she'd looked out of the small window at a sudden shemozzle on the mossy brick wall that divided the Butlers' tiny garden from a neighbour. At eye level, tails twitching, two cats perched, a young grey

female and a large black male. The female hissed and turned
to move off; the male pounced and held her. She squirmed
and spat but he mounted her and, as she twisted, he sank
his teeth into the back of her neck and held her fast. But for
the window, they were almost within touching distance
and Edie remembered a sort of pang going through her:
Oh, poor beasts ... and feeling sorry that creatures like
these could know nothing of the excitement, warmth and
emotion that human beings shared.

Why remember those cats now? So small an incident
from the past, never in her mind since then. Until now, this
moment, this night, more than thirty years later. She turned
to look at Frank humped in bed, the eiderdown pulled well
up above his shoulders, untidy spikes of grey hair bristling
the pillow.

Outside a cat howled once again.

Oh God, she thought, life's like that. Life's like an old
tom cat that gets you by the scruff of the neck and you
can't get free.

She certainly couldn't get free. Free from fish and chips.
Never had she contemplated being caught up in such a
business, putting up with the smell as well as the work. But
she was realistic; it was a way of existing. And she knew
that – work well, work methodically, buy good quality, give
fair value, and with a bit of luck, you could make out. And
they were. Stupid, at this stage, to ask for more.

She moved quietly into bed beside Frank and, in doing
so, the diamonds on her hand glinted in the lightness of the
night. Would she, she wondered, ever have accepted that
ring had she known the long trail of difficulties ahead, a
trail that had led to the stones being steamed, day and
night, in the fumes of bubbling oil? She didn't even try to
answer the question. One of her firm beliefs: *no use crying*

over spilt milk. On impulse she turned and opened the little ring-box she'd put beside her bed. But the sapphires were too much in shadow to be seen clearly. Was it her imagination, or not? – she could swear a little whiff of frying oil drifted from the open lid, like a whispering tongue, a taunt: you'll never be free of this perfume. Oh well, she thought wryly, at least it's not as bad as the old cottonseed oil of the past.

She lay ticking off tomorrow's necessities in her mind. Must remember the boys from Morgan's building site. Good boys, most of them seemed. No joke working outside. March could be bitter. The red-haired one had been the first to come in now and again, by himself, for takeaway. Then today – well, yesterday, seeing it was already Wednesday – he'd brought his mates. It had come on to rain so they had a sit-down, tucking in good and proper. As they got up to leave she'd heard the red-haired lad say, 'What'd I tell you? Best bit of grub round here. Same tomorrow, eh?' And he'd come over to the counter to give her their order and could they have it by twelve?

Indeed they could.

She settled into her pillow thinking: six good portions of hake – or six good portions of cod, whichever's best – just on twelve.

A nice lad, that one ... Tough, but nice. She was partial to red hair, anyway. And he'd said please. Polite-like. A bit of manners about the boy.

She liked a bit of manners.

Oh, I do still wish I'd had a son meself, she thought.

Or do I.

Might have taken too much after Frank's ways, easy-come charm and no stuffing. Don't make no odds even to think of it. Not now.

What a nice open face on that boy. Such a friendly grin, you couldn't help but smile.

Her eyelids dropped as she drifted into sleep, silently repeating: *six good portions … all fresh cooked … on the dot of twelve …* on her hand, at rest between the sheets, the clean ring. Bright facets in the dark, awaiting tomorrow's steam.

MY SARAH

•

Julie Rainsbury

I hate them pointing me out. I hate to hear them whispering.

'Look, then, it's Margaret. You know. Margaret Jacob. The little sister.'

I hate the looks they cast in my direction. Looks of curiosity and contempt. No sympathy now. No understanding of what happened. I've got my hair pinned up under Mother's old chapel hat. Perhaps that's why I feel so strange today. I should be used to stares by now but I've never had my hair pinned up before. It's cold sitting on this old bench and I wish that the train would come. Everyone knows you around here, that's the trouble. They nudge each other as they go past. You can't escape their eyes or their tongues. You can't escape their judgement.

I've got a new tin trunk here by my feet and new button boots too that squeak when I walk. I've sewed till my fingers are sore and my eyes ache from squinting at the stitches. Print dresses, aprons, underwear of stiff calico. All packed in my trunk. It costs a lot to go into service. The mistresses always expect you to provide everything you'll need to wear. I know I'm fourteen and grown up now but I must admit that I'm nervous. It's a long way, London, and I'm not even used to coming into Carmarthen much.

They like Welsh girls from the farms in service in London, so the Reverend Jones says. The mistresses say we work hard. Well, used to it I suppose, aren't we? I've got my letter of introduction from him in my pocket. He always was good at letters and character references, when I come to think about it. Looking back, I often think he started a lot of the trouble with his letters.

Sitting here on this hard bench and swinging my legs to keep them warm makes me think of Reverend Jones. We used to sit in his Sunday School class, Sarah and I, on hard wooden benches rather like this.

'Don't swing your legs, Margaret. It's rude to fidget,' said Sarah.

She was ten then, six years older than I was and inclined to be bossy. I didn't care. I adored her. Most people liked Sarah. She was dark-haired with a fine, pale skin and very pretty. My hair was blonde but I longed to look like her. She was clever, too.

'So sharp you'll cut yourself, my girl,' Mam used to say when she was up to her arms in washday and Sarah had exhausted her with questions and chatter.

Mam didn't mean it. She was really proud of Sarah. She was just so busy with the house and the animals to tend and us seven children to look after as well. Sarah would toss her head and watch Mam broodingly with her intense, dark eyes.

'I will not grow up to work like Mam,' she'd vow to me. 'I want to be special or I'll not grow up at all.'

Then she'd laugh and chase me out around the yard and over the fields, her long hair flying out behind her in the wind.

Our family were Chapel really, of course, but Mam didn't mind us going up to the Sunday School. Sarah enjoyed it. She was bright, as I said, and the Reverend Jones used to lend her books. She loved stories about the lives of the saints and all the trials and troubles they went through. She would read them to me when we were tucked up in our bed at night. She peered at the dim pages by candlelight, pointing the words out to me with her finger. We pulled the old quilt about our shoulders and cuddled close.

'Do you think you could be as brave as that, Margaret?' she would whisper at the end of each story.

'No, never,' I'd answer drowsily, snuggling down into the comfort of the soft, lumpy mattress. 'I could never be a saint.'

'I wish I could,' said Sarah as she blew out the light. 'I really wish I could.'

It's hard now to think back to that time when we were all on the farm. Life was happy then and I did not realise just how lucky I was until things changed. The house wasn't grand, just the normal sort of farmhouse for these parts. It lay long and low on the hillside above the Talog brook, the cowshed at one end and the living quarters for our family at the other, as is usual. In winter the rain dripped from the overhanging thatch. The damp seeped into the stone walls and up through the beaten clay floors but it was so cosy round the fire there at night, and it was home.

Dada and Mam had to work hard. There were one hundred and twenty acres to farm with only one hired hand to help. Still, Dada always had the sixty-one pounds each year for the landlord, he made sure of that. We were not well off, but we paid our way. We were a hard-working, respectable family. I dare anyone to deny that, even now.

Poor Mam, always busy with us children and the dairy and then the whole family down with scarlet fever. I don't know how she coped. I can dimly remember her, ill herself, dragging around the house and tending us all. I recollect the discomfort and the heat of the tossed bed and the stuffiness of the room, Sarah moaning and ill in bed beside me. No doctor, mind. Mam never made a great fuss or panic about illness. To have the doctor out is dear, of course, and most people avoid it if at all possible.

Sarah was never really right again after the fever. We all gradually got better and up and about. Sarah went back to school but seemed quieter, altered. She read even more than before. The next February she was ailing again with stomach pains and coughing. Sarah just lay in bed, almost in a stupor. I watched her silently from a little chair beside the bookshelves. I stroked her damp hand. She didn't want to eat much.

'Come on, cariad,' Mam would coax. 'You'll never be strong again if you don't eat, girl.'

Sarah said the food made her choke and turned her face to the wall. It was quite true that it often made her sick. Sometimes we could persuade her with a little stewed apple on a spoon or some warmed milk from the dairy, but she was eating hardly anything at all. Mam started to get really worried. It was outside her usual experience of the ways that illness went and she didn't know what to do.

'We'll have to get the doctor, Evan,' she told my father. 'I don't know how to help her. She's beginning to be really upset every time I mention food. She's had virtually nothing for a month now. She'll never get better at this rate.'

It was the end of February, I think, in 1867 when Mam despaired and called the doctor from Llandysul. Doctor Davies was puzzled. He gave Sarah some medicine for her stomach pain, which did seem to ease. She then terrified us all with severe fits which threw her body about the bed and there were also frightening times when she seemed to be quite unconscious. It was obvious to all of us that she was very ill. Indeed, after several weeks she was pale and as thin as a skeleton. The doctor visited on several occasions, for Mam was beside herself with worry, but he could offer no real explanation.

By the autumn Sarah would not take any food from Mam at all, however hard she tried to tempt her. She was a little better and quieter and had gone back to her books when she felt she had the energy.

'You'll die if you don't eat, Sarah,' I said to her one night soon afterwards in bed.

The candle flickered but Mam and Dada had not come to bed yet and Sarah was still reading. Mam was concerned and I was getting frightened myself.

'Look, lots of the saints didn't eat,' said Sarah softly, pointing to her storybooks spread out on the bed. 'Don't let them tempt me.'

Her eyes looked rather wild and I thought she must still be suffering the effects of her illness.

'That's all right,' I said comfortingly to quieten her. 'Just take a little something now and again from me. Have something, Sarah, because I love you so much and I think you're so brave.'

So it started that, to please me, she would sometimes sip a little milk from the bottle I tucked under her arm at night when no one was about. Or, when I kissed her good night, she would take a little bread or cheese from my mouth that I kept there for her. She did it to please me, you understand. She knew I loved her. I can honestly say she hardly ate anything at all. She was a wonder to me. I was healthy and always hungry and ready for food. She truly was a saint in my eyes to be determined enough to survive on so little. I thought my big sister was wonderful. I thought she could do anything.

The vicar, Reverend Jones, had been visiting too. I often

watched him trudging up the long lane to the farmhouse, more books for Sarah clasped under his arm. When Mam first told him she thought it was a kind of miracle that Sarah could survive on no food, he initially took her up very sharply indeed. There was quite a scene.

'See reason, woman!' he snapped at poor Mam. 'You cannot honestly believe this is a miracle. Either you're more stupid then you appear to be or you're deliberately trying to deceive me. I would not have thought it of you.'

Mam drew herself up, indignant and proud.

'We may not be rich,' she retorted boldly, 'but we are certainly honest. If I swear to you that, to my knowledge, my daughter is not eating then you may take my word for it. We may be simple people but so were the people we hear of every Sunday in the Bible. Why should this thing which has befallen my daughter not be a sign to the faithful? You ask us in church and chapel to believe that such wonders have happened before. You know yourself she is a good child, a religious girl.'

Mam gripped the edge of the kitchen table, such was her fury at this accusation. It was a shock to hear her answer the vicar back, I must admit, and most unlike her. She held her head up proudly as she turned on her heel into the dairy and left him standing.

The vicar shook his head angrily at me and grabbed his hat off the peg. He banged out of the house and off down the lane without a backward glance. He kept coming, though, to see how Sarah was. He would ask again if she ate anything. Sometimes he read to her. He spoke to the doctor. I could see that they were both puzzled.

'What do you think, Doctor?' asked Dada. The doctor shrugged.

'I don't know,' he said slowly. 'I cannot truly say what

her complaint is. I certainly do not know how to relieve her. I think we can only say that she is in the hands of The Great Doctor, *Y Doctor Mawr.*'

Mam and Dada looked at each other. They were convinced that something special was happening to their daughter. If an educated man like the doctor did not know how to explain the phenomenon, who were they to doubt it was miraculous?

I missed Sarah in my games about the farm. I missed her at school. She seemed so quiet, pale and ethereal now. I was scared that I would lose her. The stories of saints which she read to me were very inspiring, of course, but not very comforting in real life. The saints seemed mostly to have noble or glorious ends. They all died and went to heaven. It was very proper, but to the little girl I was then, not very happy. I did not want my sister to die. I did not want her to be a saint.

'Let me plait your hair, Sarah,' I would beg.

I was desperate to do whatever I could for her. She would indulge me. She knew it made me more content.

'Here, put in red ribbons and this comb.'

I tended her long hair like a doll's or a bride's. She let me plait ribbons into it and sometimes, for fun, we made a crown or wreath of flowers which we placed on top. Sarah smiled at my enjoyment of the game. I thought she looked lovely.

The vicar came one day as she sat in bed decked in all her finery. He was furious.

'Popery!' he shouted. 'You're dressing her up like some Catholic statue!'

He turned to Mam.

'How do you expect her to shake off this delusion if you all believe in her and adore her in this way? How can she bear to go back to her ordinary life when you make her so special?'

I did have a pang, then, I must admit. Was Sarah doing it just because she wanted to be special? I thought about it but I couldn't believe it was really that. She surely wouldn't want to go through such agony? There must be easier ways to be made a fuss of. I felt guilty for doubting her motives. Sarah called for me:

'Margaret, I'm cold!'

I went to fill her stone water bottle which always lay at her feet to warm the bed. I put hot milk into it instead of water so she could sip it if she wished. I did that sometimes. She never drank it all, just a little. Just enough, I suppose, looking back.

Fifteen months Sarah lay in bed with her books and her writing, beautiful in the ribbons which my love tied in her hair. As far as Mam and Dada knew, she neither ate nor drank at all. They said as much to the vicar when he visited. The vicar was amazed that things were continuing. I think it was at this stage that he began to change and believe in Sarah's claims. No one asked me if she ate. I was still only six years old and not considered to be of much importance. Even if they had asked, I don't think I considered the little sips of drink and bites of food that I occasionally gave her to be eating. They amounted to hardly anything at all. She took them only, I was sure, out of affection for me. I wondered at the strength of her willpower. To me it seemed to be miraculous indeed.

During all the time that Sarah had been ill the neighbours had visited, just as we would have visited their families if any one of them had been ill. Sometimes they brought gifts for Sarah. A book, perhaps, or a new shawl. Sometimes money to help Mam with the nursing. That was normal too. It was understood that such kindness would be returned if they in turn suffered sickness. It is traditional in the countryside around here. The neighbours were astounded by the length of time that Sarah had been without food, but they were convinced of the truth of it. Why should my parents lie? They were known as honest and reliable. Their child had been ill for about two years. They had made neither a great fuss nor a great secret of the fact that she did not eat. What had they to gain by deception? As Mrs Evans, the chapel house, said on her visit, 'All things are possible to God.' We had always been taught that and we believed it.

The Reverend Jones had also become convinced that Sarah was a truly miraculous case. He could find no other explanation. Our lives changed forever when he wrote his fateful letter to *The Welshman* at the beginning of 1869. As I said earlier, he had always been good at letters. We were shown it, in English, in the paper. We read it so often that, even now, I know it by heart.

A Strange Case

To the Editor of *The Welshman*

Sir – Allow me to invite the attention of your readers to a most extraordinary case. Sarah Jacob, a little girl of twelve years of age, and daughter of Mr Evan Jacob, Lletherneuadd, in this parish, has not partaken of a single grain of any kind of food whatever during the last sixteen months. She did occasionally swallow a few drops of water during the first few months of this period; but now she does not even do that. She still looks pretty well in the face, and continues in the possession of all her mental faculties. She is in this, and several other respects, a wonderful little girl.

Medical men persist in saying that the thing is quite impossible, but all the nearest neighbours, who are thoroughly acquainted with the circumstances of the case, entertain no doubt whatever on the subject, and I am myself of the same opinion.

Would it not be worth their while for medical men to make an investigation into the nature of this strange case? Mr Evan Jacob would readily admit into his house any respectable person, who might be anxious to watch it, and to see for himself.

I may add that Lletherneuadd is a farmhouse, about a mile from New Inn, in this parish.

Yours faithfully,
The Vicar of Llanfihangel-ar-Arth.

Reverend Jones's letter changed everything. It was not just our neighbours, now, who came to visit Sarah. She was famous. A man of the church had declared his faith in her. Indeed, I'm sure that at one time or another we had the whole of Carmarthen town troop through our kitchen. They would sit warming themselves before the kitchen fire after their long trudge up the hill from Pencader station. They queued in turn to see Sarah. There was no doubt she enjoyed it. I found it exciting myself. Many people left her gifts. Mam found these gifts from strangers embarrassing, different from the traditional gifts of neighbours. I can see her now, shaking her head and wiping her hands on her apron as someone tried to give her money.

'Just put it on the bed for Sarah,' she'd say politely. 'It's for Sarah, isn't it, not for us.'

Some people were more insistent.

'Treat it as payment for the use of the house,' drawled two very superior English ladies as they thrust two guineas at Mam.

What could she do? To refuse would be insulting. She slipped them afterwards into the little box in Sarah's room.

People were coming from everywhere now. Our once-quiet lanes were thronged every day with visitors. The local farm lads had a field day acting as guides. They would wait at Pencader station for the trains to come in. They had banners and notes in their hats reading 'To the fasting girl' or 'Guide for Lletherneuadd.' Most people used them and they did a brisk trade. They profited by my sister, no doubt about it.

Doctor Davies of Llandysul was now also convinced that, in Sarah, he might well be seeing a miracle. He, too, wrote to the papers confirming the honesty of my parents and the belief of all the neighbourhood. He also concluded 'that nothing is impossible in the sight of the Creator and Pre-server of all mankind.'

My parents' faith in their miraculous daughter was now absolute. All the neighbourhood agreed with them. The people who were most respected in our community, the Vicar and the Doctor, agreed with them. Important and impressive visitors from all over Wales and beyond also agreed that in Sarah we had a saint. Sarah's own conviction that she had the power to do anything increased. Sarah believed in herself. Even I believed in her. She would still please me by accepting a sip of milk here or a crumb of food there as we huddled under the blankets at night and before our parents came to bed in the same room. She took, though, even less than before. To me, even if asked, it would have seemed hardly worth mentioning. The amounts were so tiny. I too did not know how she managed to survive.

After the letters from Reverend Jones and Doctor Davies, the correspondence in the newspapers flew thick and fast. We heard about it wherever we went. People would be reading bits out to us after chapel. Dada would hear about it down at the mart. The children talked about it in school. People coming up to the house discussed the press endlessly. We felt that we'd never be at peace again. A suggestion was being spread in the national papers that the inhabitants of Wales were ignorant and credulous. It was causing a great deal of local indignation.

'What of the minister then? What of the doctor?' asked Mam crossly as she turned the hand churn fiercely in the dairy to get rid of her irritation. 'I suppose they're just ignorant peasants too, then, are they?'

It was also being stated in the newspapers that the whole thing was a fraud and that our family were just deceiving the public in order to make money. Dada was furious. He flung the latest paper into the fire in disgust.

'Let them send who they like,' he said. 'I'll be only too glad to have the matter thoroughly investigated. I swear on the Bible and on my reputation as an honest man that my daughter eats nothing at all. Nothing, I say! There is no conspiracy or trick.'

Mam nodded sympathetically. I looked at Sarah. She stared quietly at Dada for a moment.

'Don't worry, Dada. I don't need food,' she said. 'Promise now not to give me food unless I ask for it. Don't try to tempt me to eat. I don't want it.'

'Right,' said Dada, 'we'll show them!'

I watched Sarah. She went on reading her book.

Things moved fast from then on. Dada was determined that the reputation of the family and national pride should both be vindicated. A local committee was set up and they arranged that four nurses would be sent down from Guy's Hospital in London. These, it was felt, would be professional and independent witnesses. They were to watch

Sarah for two weeks and test the claims made about her. They were not to deny her food but they were not to offer it to her unless she asked for it. Sarah and my parents willingly agreed to all the arrangements.

I remember the day that the members of the committee came up the track, dark in their winter clothes, to search the bedroom. I watched as they turned the place upside down. They searched cupboards, walls, windowsills and floors for any hidden place which might contain food. Dada helped them.

'Search away. You'll find no deception here,' he said. 'We have nothing to hide.'

They found nothing.

The men lifted my parents' bed out of Sarah's room. They didn't want any of us family to go near her in case we gave her food. I was not to sleep with her any more. Mam made me up a little bed by the hearth in the kitchen.

'I'll miss being with you at night,' I said to Sarah.

My eyes filled with tears. I had never slept in a bed by myself.

'You'll be fine,' said Sarah. We'll both be fine, you'll see.'

She was calm and serene. She was sure of her power to succeed and to convince all those who doubted her.

'It's just for two weeks, Margaret,' she said. 'That's not so very long, after all.'

The committee knocked a separate front door through the thick wall into the kitchen from the yard. They wanted the nurses to be able to go to and fro to Sarah without interrupting the family and for the family not to interfere with the nurses. I looked around me. The farmhouse looked so different. It didn't even feel quite like home any more. The days were short and, in the dusk of early evening, the house brooded on the side of the hill. Waiting.

Next morning I was up early. I went to Sarah, before the nurses came, to spend some time with her. I knew I was soon to be banished to my bed in the kitchen. I brushed her hair until it shone. I tied yellow streamers of ribbon at each side of her head so that they tumbled down golden amongst her dark curls. I brought a garland of dried summer flowers for her head. She wore her best embroidered nightdress with a black jacket over it for warmth. There was a white woollen scarf about her neck and I tucked the ends of it into the jacket and fastened them with a brooch.

The nurses came. Mam took them in to introduce them all to Sarah. They chatted to her.

'You all seem such nice ladies,' said Sarah happily.

One of the nurses, Ann Jones I think her name was, spoke Welsh. I heard her reading Sarah's Bible in Welsh with her.

It was so lonely not to see Sarah but I could hear her talking to the nurses in the daytime. At night, I would peep through the wooden partition into the bedroom. I could not see Sarah. The head of the bed shielded her from the door. Two candles had been placed on the head of the bed and a nurse sat at each side of the bed watching her. The nurses were not used to the cold. They had lit a fire in the grate and sat with hot bricks wrapped in flannel at their feet. Two nurses always watched her while two slept. Day and night. Night and day.

Six days they sat there. We crept around the rest of the house, waiting. Neighbours came and went. We started to talk in whispers. Dada went out to the fields. It was quieter in the bedroom than at first. I could hear the nurses talking, but not so often Sarah's voice. I did not hear her reading aloud to them any more.

When the doctor called that evening, the nurses spoke to

him for some time. He went into the bedroom and looked at Sarah. When he came out he stood before Dada at the table.

'Well, let us end this nonsense, Mr Jacob,' he said coldly. 'I suggest we take the nurses out of here and let the girl be fed in whatever manner she was secretly fed before.'

Dada's face flushed lividly and he jumped up, sending his chair crashing onto the floor.

'We are not dishonest,' he shouted at the doctor in a fury. 'Everything we have said is true. I have promised my daughter never to give her food unless she asks for it.'

'Dada, Dada!' Sarah's voice called urgently from the bedroom.

'See, you're upsetting her now at the very mention of it,' said Dada.

He pushed the doctor aside and strode up to Sarah's bedside. Mam and I followed. Sarah was very pale in the candlelight. She looked fragile, but then, she often had before.

'Dada,' she whispered.

She looked at him and then at me. Her dry lips moved as if to form some words. In that moment I was suddenly sure that she was going to ask for some food. Her eyes flicked about the room restlessly. She looked at Mam and Dada. The doctor and the nurses. Me in my nightdress and bare feet. A neighbour, who'd just come, peeping in at the door. She sighed. Her lips stopped moving. She turned away from the anxious faces. She said nothing.

'It's alright, Sarah,' said Mam stroking her hair. 'We're all next door if you want anything. It's alright, my love.'

Sarah died three days later. December 17th, it was, just before Christmas. She died of starvation. On the last day Dada was worried about her. He popped me back in her bed to try to warm her. She was so cold, too cold for me to comfort her. I remember holding her tight but I had no food, no nice warm milk to give her.

Dad and Mam couldn't believe it. They were numb with shock.

'I'd never have suggested the watch at all, never agreed to all the conditions, if I'd thought for a moment there was any danger to my child,' wept Dada. He was broken.

As we mourned, things got even worse. They took Mam and Dada to court. They said Sarah's death was their fault. Everyone now believed that the whole thing was a deliberate fraud. They said the family used Sarah to gain fame and money. No matter now that the churchmen and doctors had believed in the miracle. No matter that the whole neighbourhood had believed in the miracle. No blame was attached to the watching doctors and nurses who knew my sister was starving to death and yet took no responsibility for giving her food. Only Mam and Dada were to be tried and found guilty in court. I was only six. No one asked me any questions and I didn't understand enough to tell them. They say Mam just buried her face in her skirts and wept when they said she was guilty. Dada was taken away shouting angrily in Welsh, 'We did not do it! We did not do it!'

I shall be glad to get away. Somewhere where no one knows me. It was eight years ago now, but no one forgets or forgives. They never will around here. Sarah knew that. I think she almost asked for food. I think she also realised suddenly the consequences if she had. All Dada's reputation gone at a stroke and the family ruined. All her fault. I believe she honestly thought at first that she could do it, you know. When she found that she couldn't, she tried to carry on. She tried for our sakes. I'm sure myself that my sister was a saint, a sort of a saint anyway, whatever they say.

POOR PLAYERS

•

Rhian Thomas

The third of October was the wrong time to visit the town.
All along the promenade, the hot-dog sellers and deck
chair merchants and seashell women had boarded up and
gone away, leaving the salt to pick at their paintwork
through another long winter. In the first sullen streaks of
morning newspaper clung damp in doorways as if waiting,
the coming day still uncertain. The houses grasped the last
shreds of night while a milk float hummed in a side street.
He stopped at the end of the promenade, hesitated for a
moment with his hand laid tentatively on the wet railing,
then moved quickly down the gritty steps.

At the bottom, he paused again, momentarily dismayed
to think how the coarse sand would claw his shoes, but he
left the last step behind him with resolve. Beneath the sea
wall the beach was empty and long and bleak, stretching
out in a wide grey curve behind him where the town washed
over it. He moved on, away from the dead eyes of the kiosks
and guesthouses, with the cold, ringing emptiness of the
sea thrashing in his ears. Recoiling inside his drab anorak,
he threw a watchful eye over the sea, glad to see that the
tide-table, specially purchased and stored away months
beforehand, had not let him down. The waves were moving
back, leaving a bright layer of water across the flat sands. It
would be hours before the expanse up ahead was cut off
again. He breathed slowly into his upturned collar, feeling

the knuckles wrapped around the heavy spade handle stiffen with cold and blocked circulation. He stopped and swung the spade up to rest across his shoulder, where the wind snapped at the black bin liner wrapped around it. Blinking, he gazed round, suddenly dwarfed against the vast, sweeping sky, wondering what in the world he was doing here. No walls to keep things in place, no lines; only the heaving sea that reaches out and takes what it pleases. But he'd let go of the railings. The last of his safe lines was left behind.

He had had no trouble finding a room for the night. The road from the station was littered with bed-and-breakfast signs, swinging from verandas, hanging in windows. Number seventy-eight, Park Mount, boasted neither a park nor a hill to stand on. Its steps led directly from the front door to the pavement. A single window-box hung by gritted teeth somewhere on the second floor. Cramming misgivings into the very back of his mind, he'd allowed himself to be scrutinised in the cold hallway, pouring out hopeful flattery until Mrs Worth's eyes lost some of their edge.

'I've always thought it was such a lovely town.' His arms ached. He wanted to put his bags down, but didn't dare. 'I travel through every day – on the train, on my way to work.' She waited, arms folded stiff across a chest strong enough to stand up to any number of unruly holidaymakers. 'I've always wanted to – to spend some time here.' She was almost satisfied. 'I've always said to myself, why bother trekking across the country for a holiday when there are such lovely places just on the doorstep, as it were?'

She had nodded, her short, brittle eyelashes blinking rapidly. He breathed, grateful for her approval. 'And so,' he finished, 'as I've got a week's holiday to visit my sister, I

129

thought, why not make it a real holiday? So I wondered – do you have a room, just for one night?'

Of course she had a room. Mrs Worth led him up the stairs, congratulating herself on her discerning clientele. This one, for instance, could be retiring before long, and might be good for no end of weekends. She gave him the front room and watched proudly as he hid his dismay and said politely, 'What a lovely view.'

As his ears started to ache with the cold, he repeated to himself, this is now. I am not dreaming. His heels sank with every step, and sand crept in over the edges of his shoes. He crossed the last of the blackened, half-buried break-waters, and then he was out on the long stretch of unbroken sand where even in summer only the least sociable holi-daymakers ventured. He was further from the town now; he saw that the headland was reinforced with concrete to support the road above. The muted roar of the waves and the slow-crying gulls filled his head from one direction, and the dull, echoing hum of the coast road from the other, and he picked his tedious path somewhere in between. This is real, it is happening.

He glanced at his watch, his last ticking prop of reality, gripping his wrist. Almost half-past seven. The bay was awash with shades of blue, the sky, daubed across with great wet watercolour clouds running at the edges, split here and there with puddles of bright light. Ten more min-utes. Now the sand was less even, twisted into gouged curves by the retreating waves, with streaking pools of water left behind. There was a salty tidemark across his leather shoes. Looking up, he saw the words 'Kevin loves Julie' scrawled in a barely convincing heart shape on a con-venient slab of concrete, and wondered where his indignation had gone. He pictured himself under painted walls at the station each morning, a little man with no surprises, neck hunched into his shoulders, unflinching against the world. Hooligans. Why did they suddenly have his sympathy? They just wanted to leave their mark somewhere, something to show that they'd lived that moment. They'd be forgotten soon enough. They'd forget … He shook himself. At seven-thirty on any ordinary Tuesday morning he would be sitting on the train, shoes polished, trousers pressed, hair combed smooth, surrounded by men who avoided sitting next to each other. Already, he could feel his peppery hair flying wild. As for the anorak – goodness only knows how it had survived his sweeping tidiness and stayed in the house so long. The tight skin of his knuckle was white where he held the spade, shot through with red in the cracks. No one would have recognised him.

As the interminably cosy evening at Park Mount wore on Mrs Worth had run out of questions. His life could only be stretched so far in polite conversation. She had already turned back to her faded magazine when he summoned the nerve to ask,

'I was hoping to take a walk along the beach in the morning. Would you – I mean, I don't suppose you might have a spade I could borrow?'

Mrs Worth's eyes were on him immediately, scouring his face for an explanation, and he withered. *In this weather?* She turned to her husband. Mr Worth watched him, and then said, with some doubt,

'You must be a bit of a biologist, then?'

'Yes, that's right,' he nodded, clutching at his lifeline gratefully, 'yes, I'm very interested in …'

They waited. He fumbled in his mind for snapshots of

himself as a child on the beach. 'Sandworms,' he whispered. They looked away. The gas fire hissed.

Mrs Worth turned back to her magazine, and mumbled something about the outhouse. Her husband gazed at him and said, 'I'm sure we can find something.'

He returned to his white room, but was afraid to sleep in case the dismal walls swallowed him up. He left the bedside light on and slept, and dreamed that the door was locked, and that the spade couldn't break it down.

The railway line ran along the beach only for a short way, but for a few seconds passengers could see right out across the sands. Strange, it was all so different from this angle. It was silent from inside a train window, where all the world was inside the glass shooting towards city streets and offices in straight, reliable lines. Now, as he lifted his face, the wind beat about his ears, rattled his trouser legs, and stung his eyes. He could taste the salt on his lips, and the air wouldn't leave him alone. He could feel it all over, driving through layers of clothing, cold and clean. They had no idea, those men on the train. To them it was only a picture, an empty picture. How often had he seen it flash by himself?

Stepping off the train in the early afternoon, at the wrong station, had been like walking in a sick dream. He had felt guilty, moving along the platform with housewives and pensioners, constantly reminding himself that there was no reason to hurry. He forced himself to stop and buy a magazine, then stuffed it into his overnight bag, knowing that he would never read it. The autumn afternoon was sodden, and threatened fog. At the station entrance the housewives and pensioners left him behind.

He looked at his watch again. Almost time. At seven

forty-two the train would run by on the headland and into the town, and men in pressed trousers and polished shoes would gaze at the sea and then look at their watches to check they were on time. Once, he had looked out of the window and seen a man alone on the beach, folded over by the wind, his back turned to the world; and even as he'd dismissed him as an eccentric and looked at his watch again, he'd envied him. To be out of that train, not to care whether it ran or not ... He sighed deeply. The clouds were dragging their torn hems across the sky and the sun spilled scattered shafts of light over the waves. He scanned the headland, then turned and walked towards the water's edge, leaving shaky, flooded footprints in the wet sand. The full force of the wind caught him in the face, taking his breath, and he walked slowly, the cold air inflating his throat. His steps threw shining beads of water off his shoes. This is real, he thought. I am here. A cold silver stream of sunlight crept along the horizon, and the last trickle of the waves' onslaught washed safely around his feet. Very soon now. He tightened his eyelids against the sun, and threw his gaze all around. They would be able to see him here. A corner of the black bin liner had worked itself loose from the spade, and the wind tugged and swept it like a banner, an emblem. His shoulder ached. Not long ...

From somewhere in the distance the railway tracks rang with the rush of a train. He drew himself up straight and as tall as he could. The wind froze his face, and he could feel the colour on his cheeks. The sound grew stronger, mingling with the persistent traffic and the numb fire of the waves. Louder. It would almost be in sight now; but he stood straight, facing the sea, feeling the wind laugh at his thinning hair. His ears were burning with cold, and the freezing air ached inside his head. The thundering rattle of the train rang out over the beach. Were they watching? Little men with no surprises, little men whose eyes he avoided every morning; he wanted them to watch. The sound was brimming through the clouds, beating at him with the wind, and he swayed and stood his ground. *Look: there's someone on the beach. And – something over his shoulder?* His hands ached with ice in the bone. Were they watching? Did they see him stand?

The roar died away as the train wound its way into the town, echoing under the bridge and between the quietly waking houses. He lifted the spade from his shoulder, bending slowly to let it rest on the sand. The gulls spiralled dolefully overhead, crying for the unrest of the sea and the sky. Pressing his fingers to the warmth of his neck, he felt the slow tingle of blood moving beneath the skin. There was a dark ship waiting beneath the shadowy horizon. He could make out its angular outline against the grey sea; so far away. The cold, bright glare of the early sun retired, and the day began. The rumble of traffic on the coast road grew more frequent as he stood, the waves a little further down the sand. The bin liner clung about his wet feet. It was a long walk back to town.

LOVEY-DOVEY CATS' EYES

•

Jacqueline Jacques

I couldn't turn to close the gate, look, speak. Could not. My face ached with polite smiling, while my eyes were blind with tears. The drive home was a blur.

That such people exist! But you never would have guessed. She was small and harmless, a wee country mousie who seemed to have become stuck in a time warp. I placed her lank hair and ankle-length skirts somewhere in the mid-seventies. And she wore those granny specs that John Lennon used to have, making me think that she might be someone with insight, with imagination. Ha!

Coming from my tiny flat, I wasn't prepared for something even smaller. When I had to duck through the cottage doorway I felt like Alice in the White Rabbit's house, growing steadily bigger.

I said to her, 'This place wasn't built for people reared on school milk and cod-liver oil.'

'Can't swing a cat,' she agreed.

But despite its lowly dimensions it was a lovely room. The plastering was recent but the timber frame, black with the touch of a hundred ghostly hands, was old, old, old. I saw myself in the summer months, making bundles of the herbs and flowers that I would grow in the garden, and hanging them to dry from the ceiling joists. Very Laura Ashley. And I lusted after that log fire, with a cat sprawling on the rag rug before it, or maybe perched on the window seat, yattering at the birds being blown about outside. I told her of my dream of retirement, with a cat as my companion. Pets aren't allowed in the flats where I live. Lovers and ghosts, but not animals. Which is why I was moving.

'*I* have cats,' she said.

I looked around but could see none; I thought I'd probably spooked them when I came in.

I wouldn't need to dump all my knick-knacks, I thought. There were nooks aplenty to display them. I caught the glint of my brasses, mounted on the white walls, reflecting firelight or the sun in the afternoon. Oh, it would be just right. Already I had thrown out her old table and rickety bentwood chairs, her sad sideboard, her heavy armchair, and installed my new beechwood bookshelves and matching units, my Cintique suite, and my desk. It could go under the window where Miss Mousie had her sewing machine. From the mess of material and wadding and foam rubber heaped on the table it seemed that I had interrupted a morning's dressmaking.

'What are you making?' I asked her, 'something for the new house?'

'No, no,' she said, 'would you like to see?'

And she lifted a shroud of flowery stuff from the machine and my heart stopped. Whatever do you think? A tiny child's body lay there, not moving, its hand impaled by the silver needle. 'Oh!' I said. It took me a moment to realise that the child was not in pain.

'A doll,' she said, fondly. 'I make dolls.'

Of course. When I looked closer I could see flesh-coloured stitching and flesh-coloured seams. A doll. A beautiful child doll, so cleverly fashioned as to be almost lifelike. Little curled hands, a triangular mouth, slightly open, and lovey-dovey cats' eyes, wide and unblinking. And the blue towelling sleep-suit. Perfect. I couldn't help myself, I had to stroke it, as you would a real baby, the smooth round contours of its little body. And froze! It was perfect in *every* detail.

'Anatomically correct,' she informed me. 'I do Mums and Dads, too, the whole extended family, in fact. They're teaching aids for kids.'

I noticed that there was dried spittle at the corners of her mouth.

I told her that I'd seen them on television, used with children in abuse cases. The kids felt more inclined to act out their traumas with dolls than to confess their 'secrets' to inquisitive strangers.

'Oh, the dolls have no end of uses,' she said. 'It's better to work out your hang-ups or your aggressions or even your fantasies in private, by playing with inanimate objects, than to run the risk of damaging someone in real life. Counsellors and therapists use them all the time, to release inhibitions, and they're a good way of teaching people with learning difficulties ... about things like sex and HIV and what-have-you.'

(Toy condoms, I thought, whatever next?)

But the idea of spending your days fashioning tiny private parts from flesh-coloured cloth gave me the creeps, no matter how worthy the cause. I was glad to pass on to the next room.

The kitchen was pocket-sized but organised, with gadgets galore, to suit a busy woman. She explained that there had been a man, twenty-odd years ago, but that he had gone to India, seeking enlightenment, and had died from drugs and dysentery. Since then she had made her own way, in soft toys. She had contracts with several educational suppliers. Now it was time to expand the business, find larger premises. All this as we were mounting the ladder-like staircase. At the top, as I was stooping to avoid braining myself on a low beam, she told me that in order to fit in a bathroom she had had to split her second bedroom in two, though she had hated having to do it.

She hoped that I was not one of those people who desecrated old property in order to make a fast buck.

'It's all they can think of: extending here, exposing there, knocking this down, gutting that. Then they sell it for a fortune, buy up some other wonderful old building and proceed to knock the history out of that!' A woman with a conscience, clearly.

I didn't tell her that, the moment her last seamy puppet was stowed on the van, I intended to perform a little cosmetic surgery of my own: just a face-lift and tummy tuck to bring back the roses round the door. I had Snow White's cottage in mind: wooden shutters with heart-shaped cutouts, stable doors, a white picket fence and a couple of Walt Disney bluebirds simpering on the windowsill.

Her bedroom was tent-shaped. The wind was roaring in the thatch and I could hear the scrabble of tiny animals on the ceiling as they burrowed deeper into their haven for warmth. The room was so small and crowded that the hand-worked quilt crept out onto the landing.

They sat stiffly, their mouths like an 'O', registering surprise. Her 'extended family' ranged along the wall-length shelves, on the windowsill, on the rafters. They tumbled over the bed in impossible positions. They spilled onto the floor in an orgy of extravagance.

'So you don't sell them all?' I asked.

'Oh, I like to keep some around me. After you've put so much work into them they become old friends. No two are alike, you know.'

Nor were they. They were ethnically correct as well, in all shades, all sizes. Some of the men had moustaches, some wore glasses. But they all had lovey-dovey eyes and a sort of family likeness. And then I saw whose genes they had inherited. On a shelf beside the bed was his photo. Beneath the beads and flowers and the flowing hair, the lovey-dovey cat's eyes of the errant boyfriend. Poor Miss Mousie.

She stood on the landing while I paid homage to the bath and WC. There wasn't room for two. And then, next door along, was the bathroom's other half. In it were three cages and in each of the cages was a cat. A living, breathing, silent, withdrawn, indifferent cat. She took one out to show me, a black and white tom with haunted yellow eyes; she draped it over her arm, stroked it until it purred and then she put it back.

'Do you breed cats?' I asked.

'No, I don't breed them.'

'Do you show them?'

'No.'

'Why do you keep them up here?'

'Cats and sewing don't mix,' she smiled. 'They'd rip my dolls to rags. Besides, there are pins and things. I love cats and I'd hate anything to happen to them.'

In the garden, among the winter jasmine, was another cage. 'For when it gets hot,' she said.

CHARITY

•

Clare Morgan

At the wedding she had said 'Yes,' and 'until death'. That was a long time ago and her hair was quite grey now, and her eyes were marooned in a sea of little wrinkles.

Alessandro saw them, the eyes and the wrinkles, when he knocked at her door. She was a typical, timid woman who answered his knock, too many years without a man, too many days and nights in the long bed (bought to accommodate her husband, surely, because she was a very short woman), alone.

Alessandro held out the collecting box, and seeing the refusal begin to form in her, the tensing of the muscles in her neck and the start of the side to side movement of her head that would send him back down the steps empty-handed, he said,

'It's a good cause.'

What he really said was,

'Ees a good cau-sa,' because he found English difficult, having only recently, and reluctantly, given up a long-standing career at sea.

'I deen wanna,' he said to his one friend Elis, who was also an exile, having settled by accident in the county after spending most of his life in the North.

'I deen wanna.' But what else, his accompanying shrug seemed to indicate, can a man do?

'Ees a good cau-sa,' he repeated, standing on her top

step with the wind that funnelled up the street, and before
that, up the valley that became the street, lifting the blunt
ends of his straightish hair.

He shook the collecting box and the coins inside rattled.
The wind brought with it the smell of living in a strange
place. He knew many of the smells of the different places in
the world. Rio, Santiago, Durban, Quattar. Now he smelled
the particular smell of this small part of a small country. It
had nothing to do with politics. The smell of a place was
made up of its weather and its history. That was how he
wanted to think of it. It wasn't as simple as that but he
wished it to be simple, because he had led a complicated
life and it had tired him, and now he wanted to lead a
simple life, and feel the tiredness leave him, and sense himself to be at peace.

He shook the box again and said,

'Anything ...'

She moved her head from side to side, very firmly this
time, with just the right balance of decision and condescen-
sion, lengthening her neck a little so that the large lapels of
her flowered blouse could assert themselves.

'No,' she said, in a soft voice that was definite too. He
thought that she had probably been a schoolteacher. Either
that, or a district nurse. He could imagine her quelling unruly children with a look. He could imagine her too in
uniform, closing her front door at dawn or before dawn,
pulling it to behind her with a click and getting into her
dark little car and feeling the hem of her gabardine raincoat
rasping her stockings as she adjusted her legs.

He was going to say something more to try to persuade
her but she had already closed the door, almost, and the
only thing that was left of her was an eye.

And what an eye it was, he said to himself afterwards,

walking along with the collecting box hanging by its two strings from his wrist. It was an eye that was ageless and placeless. It was Eve's eye. It was the eye of every woman he had made love to, and of most of those he had fucked.

Alessandro (it was a nickname, he had been baptized Jesus José) was widely experienced in women. He had fucked women in most of the countries of the world. He had made love to women rather more selectively, perhaps in only two or three countries. There had been a few boys too, Morocco had been bad that way, for temptation, but he did his best to forget about those experiences. There were things it was better not to let in, they cluttered up your life, they made it difficult for you to be at peace.

That evening, when he was sitting on the bench by the war memorial waiting for Elis (it was a warm enough June, and girls with their legs all bare and little cotton tops that their breasts pushed out of were walking up and down) he thought of the woman again. She was fifty, or more than fifty. He thought of her body and knew what it would be like, because he had measured the decay of his own. He had measured the decay and hated it. His own age, other people's age; he hated the fact that youth was naturally fuckable and age was not. If he had been a different kind of man he would have taken to drink. As it was he confined himself to moderation and maintained a certain terseness in his dealings with his inner and regretful self.

When Elis came he asked him who the woman was, knowing already, because he had asked at the shop, that she was Miss Thomas, Gwynfryn. She was a relative newcomer and kept very much to herself.

'They say she came from Pontypridd,' Elis said. 'But then, I've heard too that she came from Abergavenny.'

Elis said it rather mournfully. He was a mournful man, recently widowed. There was loneliness in the angle of his cap. They sat on the bench talking quietly and irregularly for half an hour or an hour, watching but not watching the girls walking up and down, and the boys who sat on the wall together and swung their legs, and pushed their hair back off their foreheads and then, after a suitable interval, let it fall forwards again.

The only thing left of her was an eye. It was the eye that he remembered throughout the following day, as he went from house to house with his legs getting heavier and his heart feeling large under his ribs.

'A good cau-sa,' he said, again and again. And most of the men and women agreed.

At the end of the afternoon he climbed the steps to the Town Hall and went in past the Corinthian pillars (too grand entirely for the building, and the building itself too grand for the town, but that was how they had done things in the old days. You could see it in all the big old buildings, the sense of getting ahead of yourself, the idea of some-where big and important where, with a little effort, anyone could go).

He offered his collection box to be counted and sat down to wait. The room, which was a large room with high ceil-ings and a cornice, contained, as well as the tables where people were counting out the money, displays of all the uses the place had been put to over the years. There were photographs of it turned into a hospital during the war. Then in the first war, as a recruitment office. Alessandro recognised a picture of Kitchener. Then there was a faint, yellowy-looking photograph, the steps packed with people and a banner with Welsh words on it that he couldn't understand, and a banner with English words that he could.

'That,' Elis said when he asked about it later, 'was the investiture of the Prince of Wales. Nineteen hundred and two, I think it was. Anyway, a long time ago.'

Then there was tea, at the Coronation. A party for the Silver Jubilee. Brass band competitions. The crowning of Miss Miskin, a plain little girl with hair straggling on her shoulders. A rally, during the miners' strike. Boxing contests, and wrestling, on a Saturday afternoon.

The wrestling held Alessandro's interest. The other pictures had bored him. It was not, after all, his country, and all the pictures seemed to be of grey, indistinguishable faces. But the last picture of all was of two women wrestling, and it held his attention because it reminded him that once two prostitutes had pretended to fight over him. He had forgotten, because it was a long time ago, exactly where. Perhaps it had been one of the Mediterranean ports, but he thought not. It had more the feel of South America to it. Anyway, they had pretended to fight over him, and his shipmates had been envious. He couldn't remember which of the women had won. One had been darker than the other. One had been very thin. Had the dark one been thin? Or had the thin one had lighter hair, almost a reddish kind of colour, which grew down onto her forehead in a peak? It was odd how you remembered, sometimes, the littlest of things. Afterwards he'd had both of them, the first in a proud way, offering his body as a kind of prize. The second he'd treated more gently, feeling for an instant an unfamiliar desire to console.

He hadn't thought about it from that day to this. But he thought about it now, and it made him restless, and he leaned forward and looked at the photograph closely, the one woman fleshy and blonde-looking and with a lot of black stuff around her eyes, the other darker and more wiry altogether, with her hair cut off short around her face, and a defiant look as she stared at the camera, the corners of her mouth pulled in tight. 'Mad Marge' the caption under the photograph said. 'Mad Marge v. Jinny the Giantess. September 1963.'

And when I said 'Yes,' Marged said (going to the window and looking out to where the grass was growing on the landscaped part, very green indeed all the way up the hill, but too smooth to be a real hill, and with a few black bits showing, however much they tried to hide them, in between).

When I said 'Yes,' I hadn't meant yes in the way people mean it, the forever kind of yes that lives with you and becomes part of you and you can't get away from. I meant the *for now* yes, this minute, today, this week. But yeses had a habit of catching you. Noes were safer. And all that time ago she'd said Yes, just for the sake of it, really.

'Marged,' he'd said, looking very sorry for himself one night, sitting in her Mam's back kitchen on the way home from the pub. And she'd said, almost without meaning to, it was strange when she heard herself say it,

'Very well, Ifor.'

It was a grown-up thing to say.

And after they were married he stood at the foot of the bed and took his clothes off, one by one, his tie, his shirt, his socks, his underpants (she had looked the other way when he unbuckled his belt). He had stood at the foot of the bed, at last with nothing on at all, and his body rather thin and drab, and a thin streak of shadow under the curve of every rib, and almost directly under the electric light, so that his body looked elongated a little, although it cast no shadow, which was strange because everything else in the room had a rather black shadow attached to it. When she had seen him like that she knew the true nature of the mistake she had made, and knew also that it was not something she could put right, not ever, because now she had done it it was part of what she was, and your self was one thing you couldn't get away from, no matter how long or how earnestly you tried.

In the event, it was Ifor who had got away from her. Not that even that was true, really. He had never been hers, although he might have liked to be. And she had certainly never been his, except in the exchange of her body for his name, and in doing the things a wife does, like a maid really. Her mother had been a maid before the war, up at Canal Head House, Marged had seen a photograph of her with her hands clasped in front of a little white spoon-shaped apron, and another little bit of something white, with primped-up edges and a visible kirby grip, settled precariously in her hair.

'Ifor not back for the weekend?' her next-door neighbour Eirianfa said. (Eirianfa came from Dolgellau originally, and went back there not long after. The South never really suited her, it was impossible to settle, somehow, in the strange, pale air.)

'Ifor not back?'

Marged had said to herself when she was a child that she would never be anybody's maid. There was an old snapshot, quite bent around the edges, of her in a sunbonnet, staring out fiercely from the deep shade the brim cast across her face. She was waving a stick at the camera, and the little cluster of lumps that was her knuckles stood out.

'Fierce, by God,' Ifor had said when she showed it to him, the only time, really, she had showed him anything.

The way he said 'Fierce' troubled her. He said it with that look she didn't like in men, the mouth too relaxed, and the pupils of his eyes taking on a dark look, and the muscles in the neck tightening and then going slack again.

When Ifor had left, eventually, not letting her know beforehand, just not coming back, and getting a friend to write her a letter, an English friend, they were working on the new road near Ross (the letter had a Hereford post-mark), when Ifor had left she felt strange, and separate, and missed for a few nights the idea of him taking his socks off at the bottom of the bed.

'Ifor not back, then?'

Ifor will never be back. Ifor will never lift the latch on the gate, and take the three steps you have to take to get to the door, and open it, and come in, bringing with him the smell of the outside, the town in his coat and in his hair, the smell of the exhaust fumes, the cold wind under his finger-nails.

Behind the house where she had a room, in Cardiff, in a small street that didn't lead anywhere, was a dug-up piece of earth with primroses on one side and daffodils on the other, and the brown-coloured bits of what was left of the snowdrops in between. (My life has been made up of back yards, and half-turned earth. And the walls of the houses going up very straight, and the roofs, in layers, angling back over themselves.) There was a lot of traffic and the shop windows were very shiny and you saw, as you went past them, your own reflection coming at you from differ-ent angles. It didn't seem like you. You were no longer the person you had thought you were, but another person who looked rather like you but wasn't. (And what is this strange sense every morning, waking up, of my self getting smaller and smaller, like an island in the middle of a river rising in flood?)

'You,' the man said, and pointed at her, there, in a line, waiting to see if you were any good at it, looking at you first as you walked up and down in a swimming costume, looking at you very closely indeed as you waited, your turn three away, then next-but-one, then next, and the others already there and doing it, or having done it, the grunting and the falling, the pretending, and the odd occasional blow that caught you like a fiery and exploding thing.

The man's forefinger was stiff and straight at the end of his straight arm.

'You!' The finger moved twice, from the joint.

She stepped forward. She felt like a schoolgirl. She felt as she had done sometimes in chapel, on a Sunday. If there had been any excuse for it, that would have been different. If she had done it for any of the reasons women do things, any of the old reasons –

'You!' the man said.

And then she stopped thinking about it and climbed up, with big, fluid movements, into the ring.

Now, Marged. What was it like? (looking out over the landscaped part and counting the black bits: one, two, three, four, see how they all link up and make a pattern, like veins the black bits are, snaking in and out of the green).

When she had first come there, nearly thirty years before, everything had been black still. The wheel had been turning, the spokes of it all in a blur. Strange how memory took away the colour. The sky had been white. She had climbed up into the ring and felt the top rope scrape at the skin of her shoulder, and the middle rope press into the flesh of her thigh and then spring loose again as she let it go. She had stood up in that square free space that took away entirely and for the allotted time her freedom, and felt cut off from everything that she knew and was, from everything that she had ever dreamed of, or wanted to be. And yet how solid the sweat had felt running down her back, and down her ribs at the sides under her arms. How real the faces were still, and the room, hot and tight on her, and the air thick with the tail ends of words. She never knew for certain whether she had been more herself at those times, or less.

'Stick to what you know,' her mother had urged her once, fiercely, although her voice was getting very thin. But sometimes knowing (she had come to understand) can be more of a burden than a relief.

And what do I truly know? (staring in the mirror in the room in Cardiff, with her back to the window, and the patch of earth unturned now behind her, and treacly-looking in the uncentred light).

What do I truly know?

There had been a man she went to bed with sometimes, but intermittently. His body had been solid and his steps definite on the linoleum as he collected up his clothes. And something in it had brought her afterwards back to this half-known place, rather like Eden, the old pictures of it, sketches in Borrow, *Wild Wales*. Eden no longer. (She had heard her mother speak of the boy from Canal Head House riding his pony up on Ferndale, late in the afternoon.)

And yet it was in a way like Eden. Quiet, her house. Peaceful before the fall. The clock ticked. The flames in her gas fire made little whiffling noises when the wind backed round. She had pointed herself, like a weather vane, in this inevitable direction. She did not long for, she resented rather, the sound of a step on her step, the rasp of the knocker, tentatively yet deliberately raised.

Who is it? she called, in her head perhaps, because it was evening now and the children who played outside in the street had gone in, and a certain thickening in the outline of things told you it would soon be dark.

Who is it?

Alessandro took his hands out of his pockets. The edge of his pockets rasped over his knuckles as he withdrew his hands. A cool current of air wound up the street towards him and threaded itself between his ankles and slid up over his shoulders and around his neck. He put his head on one side at an awkward angle and looked up past the dark shape of the hill rising away. The sky was a colour he had never seen before. It was the colour he thought it would be the first time he crossed the Equator. A dark, indescribable colour. He settled his weight back on his heels. Something ticked inside him, like a metronome. The street, where it fell away quite steeply, was dull under the lack of stars. A light came on inside the house, and went out again. He felt the wind lodge in a series of cold little bars under his fingernails. The town was yellow now below him, the hill black and solid-looking behind. He wondered whether he should knock again. He strained for a sound of something inside the house, but there was only the wind out there with him, and the curious half darkness lapping the promontories of his hands.

TWO CHILDREN

•

Danw November

The elder boy. The younger girl. It is summer. Late summer. The sand comes in her shoes. The shoes are heavier and heavier and drag at her feet.

'Wait a minute, Ge-o! I take my shoes off.'

'You'll lose them, nipper. Don't take them off!'

But she picks up the pumps, pours the hot sand out and over her toes, spreads her toes apart and watches the grains slip through. Then she marches on behind Geo, clasping the pumps, sand pushing up between her toes.

'The sand gets in your toes,' she laughs.

'Come on, slowcoach!' he calls over his shoulder, striding on ahead of her on his skinny seven-year-old legs.

'I hurry!' and she pants up to his side.

They pass along the wide sandy track. Past the lagoon they walk, where on other days they go out in bright-coloured blue, green and red boats and explore the mysterious distances of the Mere. They walk alongside the silent Sunday boathouse. The boatman who smokes his pipe is not there today. Further on, the road widens and there is a pool with willow trees and a curtain of emerald slime wrinkled across it from side to side. Keep away! warns her mother, when they go past together.

Up further are the little wooden houses and their tiny worlds of gardens – in this one a rabbit, who eats all the lettuce you can stuff her with, in that one a slowcoach of a tortoise who is bigger than any tortoise Hellie has ever seen, with a great shell like crazy paving and curved like a cave. The tortoise can hide her head in there somewhere, and hisses if she is angry. That proves she is a reptile, together with her scaly skin, her darting tongue, her hibernation in winter, says Hellie's mother. Then why does she eat grass? wonders Hellie, who believes all reptiles are like boa constrictors and want to eat people.

The two children carry on and turn up a rough stony track that leads inland, past the last few houses and wooden fences and weedy gardens and untidy hedges. Suddenly through a gate they are up high where they can see across the sea.

'Where are we?' asks Hellie.

'Don't worry, nipper – you won't get lost with me,' replies her brother. He charges on ahead, while Hellie stumbles painfully with tender feet on sharp stones. And she is getting too hot in the sun. Her face is flushed.

'I want a drink,' she calls. She runs up to Geo, pulls at the bottle he carries. But Geo pulls away from her and out of reach of her eager hands. He carefully unscrews the bottle top and gulps the water into his throat.

'I asked for it. I asked first,' she screams, red in the face with anger.

'Shut up, nipper! You can have it now. Look: it's not so full. But watch it! Don't get your tongue stuck in the bottle!'

'Will my tongue get stuck in the bottle?' asks Hellie, frightened to put the bottle to her lips. When she does, the water runs all down her front.

'Fathead!' jeers her brother. 'Look – like this!'

But Hellie won't let him hold the bottle for her, in case he is up to one of his tricks. She ends up going thirsty.

They walk on a bit. There are thorny hedges on either side of the track. Occasionally they see great horned cows and young bullocks. Geo decides to explore one of the fields they are passing. They climb over the five-barred gate. There is thick, dry mud where the cattle have tramped and pushed against the gate. There is no more sand here. But still Hellie won't put on her shoes.

'Where are you taking us?' she asks. He doesn't bother answering. He rushes on ahead again while Hellie trails behind. They cross the wide field and run past some noisy, watchful cows with muddy legs and big flapping udders.

'That's a moo-cow, Hellie,' says Geo.

'I know,' she replies. 'I'm not just a baby.'

Through another field they travel, and another, and past a dropaway cliff on their right.

'Careful!' warns Geo. 'Hold my hand, nipper!'

'I'm not a nipper,' she complains, getting cross and feeling suddenly tired and thirsty as well.

Now the fields are all edged with empty space. Gulls sometimes fly to meet them here, rising on beautiful breezes that buoy them up from the sea's margin.

Then ahead of them they see the barbed wire.

'What's that?' asks Hellie, pointing.

The barbed wire extends as far as they can see, beyond the next gate, loosely rolled and tangled and spreading out along the clifftop. There are no more hedges here, just a wide desert full of barbed wire, a maze with no pathways.

'Let's go and explore!' cries Geo, excited, grabbing Hellie's hand and pulling her along till they stand at the gate.

'I'm too tired,' she complains, 'I don't want to go there. I want to go home now, I do.'

But Geo doesn't hear her. He jumps up and over the gate. Then he hesitates a moment, casts his eye over the plunging cliff, then back to his sister. Then he begins to make his way into the maze.

Hellie is slow to follow. She puts her sandshoes down. Gingerly she climbs up the great gate. She clambers to the top, fearful but too proud to call to Geo for aid. At the top she bends low. Her chin touches the top rung. She lifts one leg over, as her mother taught her. Now she sits astride and looks around her.

To the left, the land they have walked upon looks kind and familiar. To her right, shimmering in the unshaded heat, the wire winks and shines as it winds away and away.

'Why is Geo so bossy?' she wonders. 'Why do I always have to do what he wants?'

He is waving at her now, turning round and waving, from inside that web of wire.

'Come on, slowcoach! We can play soldiers in here. Bang, bang! You're dead if you don't take cover. I'm the Germans and I'm going to kill you. You're a sitting duck on that gate.'

But still she lingers, looking back. She looks beyond Geo where the barbed wire stretches to the very horizon. What sort of a place is this? A wilderness? A minefield? A rifle range?

Whatever it may be, Hellie feels foreboding. She glances down to the sea below her – away from the menacing field. Her eyes focus on an abyss, a great chasm full of the boom of breakers and the wail of gulls. It is bright, glittering, hot and hard with the afternoon sun. And fearful, ominous.

Hellie turns, lifts her other leg over the gate, carefully climbs down, turns again and runs to catch up with her brother.

She forgets that she has left her sandshoes, neatly placed side by side, at the bottom of the gate. On the other side.

'I'm thirsty. Mutti! I want a drink.' And she reaches up to

her mother, who touches her hair, strokes the little girl's head nervously, and says nothing.

'My hand hurts. They hurt my hand. They hurt my finger. Mutti! My hand!' cries the boy.

At length the woman bends down to him. She is shocked and disoriented. She finds it hard to respond to her two children. Anyway, what can she do? At length she comes to her senses and finds words to reassure them.

'I want to go home now, Mutti,' says the little girl.

'Quiet, Isaac darling! Hush Helena my childling! Mutti will look after you, sweethearts. Look, Isaac, you will feel better very soon. See what Mutti is making for your hand!'

She pulls up the hem of her dress. She tears at her petti-coat beneath, putting her teeth to it. She tears a jagged piece of cloth from it. This she puts to her mouth, screwing up her face and chewing it and wetting it with her saliva. When it is thoroughly wet, she tears it in two pieces. With one piece, she binds up the boy's wounded hand, winding the rag round and around the finger and then around the hand. She tucks the end in and under.

'Hold that firm! Don't let go!' she orders him.

They are standing in a queue, waiting.

'What for are we waiting?' asks Isaac.

'For the train to come,' says his mother.

'Why don't we get a drink? I want a drink. I'm thirsty. Mutti!' wails the little girl.

'See here! I'm making you lovely and cool now, Helena,' says her mother, spitting into the other piece of rag and wiping it over the child's forehead and cheeks and dry, cracking lips.

'Hold this to your head now, Helena!'

It is mid afternoon. The sun is at its hottest. There is no

shade for them. The woman tries to shelter her children with her shadow, standing between them and the glare.

'Poor little daughter! The air is so hot for you, with your tender skin,' murmurs the mother.

'How long will we wait now? For the train?' asks the weary girl, cuddling against her mother's skirts.

'O very, very soon now it will come. Very soon. And then ...'

'Where is it taking us? Will we be in prison, like Tante Rachael?' asks Isaac.

'No, dear one. Tante Rachael had bad ideas and that is why they took her away. Where we are going we shall be safe, safe from people with bad ideas. They are taking us away from our enemies, Isaac.'

'Will the train take us home?' asks Helena.

'O no,' says her mother. 'Better far than going home. We're going on a journey. Far away, to a better land. Who knows: perhaps so much better, it will be like long ago, full of milk and honey ... remember?'

'Like long ago and the Prophets?' asks Isaac.

'Like long ago and the Prophets.'

'Tell us again! Tell us again the story, Mutti, of the land of milk and honey!' asks Helena.

And the mother sits down on the platform and draws the two children to her. In the middle of the restless, moaning queue of wretched people she tells her story.

'Once, long ago, our people lived in exile. And they lived always with a promise: the promise of the Promised Land ...'

And she retells her story, like so many times before. Over and over the same words the children know, the words full of familiarity and comfort, until the girl and the boy fall asleep.

The woman lifts them one by one and moves them back to a handwagon nearby. She places them against its side, with care, so they are in its shelter. Isaac still clutches the rag that his mother gave him. Helena too.

Her mother removes the little girl's wooden clogs and places them neatly, side by side, just under the wagon. Then she herself sits down to rest, leaning across their bodies, her head and arms resting on the wagon. She is asleep instantly.

'What is this for?' asks Hellie, timidly touching one of the strands of barbed wire.

'Don't touch!' warns Geo. It's been here ages. Years and years. Ever since the Germans tried to invade. They came over the sea in planes. Wheeee ... poooow!'

'And who put it there?'

'The soldiers did. They put it there to get the Germans in a muddle. So if they landed then they'd get stuck in it and couldn't get any further.'

Hellie turns round and around. The hostile strands bar her way.

'I want to go home now,' she murmurs, scared and lost.

'All right,' replies Geo.

But they can't find the way they came. Every way they go, they get more and more lost. The sun gets hotter and hotter. It is mid afternoon. The sun is at its hottest.

Hellie starts to cry.

'I tell you what,' says Geo, trying to be brave, 'we'll sit down and have another drink and we can be the soldiers in the desert and this is a bottle of brandy. And I've been injured in the battle, and then we look at our ... compass. And then we find the way. OK?'

So they sit down right where they are and Hellie lets

Geo give her the water, holding the bottle for her so she doesn't spill it.

As far as their eyes can see it is all glimmering heat and dry dust and tufts of grass and flowerheads gone to seed in the blaze of August. And miles and miles of barbed wire, barring their way.

'Now you lie down and pretend to be asleep and I look at my compass,' orders Geo.

Hellie stops crying and lies down. She is immediately asleep. Geo practises winding and unwinding strands of barbed wire until he gashes his finger. He cries out and Hellie stirs. But she doesn't wake. He watches the blood and then pulls up some fat herb leaves which he twists round and around his finger to stop the blood. He remembers his mother doing that before.

Geo takes a swig of water and lies down beside his sister. Soon he too is fast asleep, his head upon the bottle. One hand holds the other, pressing on the herbs to keep them in place.

'Stand up! Stand up!' shouts a fierce and booming voice.

The woman blinks her eyes open, pulls herself up, shields her two sleeping children. A baton hits her legs. She winces but does not cry out. The ones that cry out always get hit again. She puts her hand across her eyes to shade them from the sun's glare. People all around her are bustling about, collecting things up, smoothing down their clothes, trying to tidy their hair, soothing their children. They are on the move at last.

'Children also,' orders the same voice.

The woman stoops and shakes them awake. The soldier passes up the queue.

She sets the girl and boy on their swaying legs. The sun is burning hot. Isaac is looking pale. Helena starts to cry. She puts her arms out for her mother to pick her up. But the woman ignores her.

'Shush your tears!' she commands. Hearing the fear in her mother's voice, Helena goes suddenly silent.

'You are from a respected family. We do not show fear. And we never submit. Not in our hearts. Remember this!

'Helena, put on your clogs! See, there they are! Isaac, show me that wound!'

The guards hustle the queue along the platform, far too narrow for all this crowd of people. The platform leads down to cattle-trucks at the far end. The woman sees great doors opening up before her eyes: stifling and dark and hot as hell. Surely not those! They won't have to travel in those?

Now the curt, cruel voices are roaring at them to hurry.

'Move on! Into the trucks! We haven't got all day you know.'

The queue turns from human beings to mindless bodies, bodies without names any more. Trying to keep hold of bags, bundles, children, babies – pushing and being pushed – the nightmare crowd crushes into the trucks. More and more are thrust in behind the first.

No one would guess how many suffering beings could be held in those stinking caverns, nor for how many days they would be crushed together like this, without food, without water. The woman, still cradling her boy's hurt hand, is torn away from him. She is carried along on the tide of bodies, hurled away from the children. She ends up in a truck against a wall of flesh.

'My boy! My babies! Isaac! Helena!' she screams, losing control. A man next to her mutters:

'Better off out there, woman, than in this hell. What good are you to them now?'

The boy and girl are thrown down hard against the concrete platform as the people surge over them, harried on by the guards, into the trucks. Isaac somehow grabs hold of Helena. Beneath the heave of bodies and the kicking of wooden clogs and leather boots he shouts to her:

'Hold your head, little sister! Hold your head!'

And he even tries to grasp her tiny dimpled fists and guide them to her head, to protect her skull from battering boots. In the rush and crush of bodies the two children are thrown back against the handwagon. The crowd passes over them and leaves them behind, bruised, concussed.

All of a sudden Isaac is picked up and hurled into a truck. The doors boom shut and grip him tight between suffocating bodies and hard unyielding boards. The dark is stifling, thick with sweat and fear. He is choking for air. He urinates in terror. He hears his own mother crying for him somewhere in the dark and is too short of breath to answer.

The sun is still hot: very hot. But it is past the zenith and the ground gives back more heat than the sun above. A patch of mud creaks as it cracks open, dry and gaping like a dead mouth. A seed pod bursts open: crack! All across the waste land, the heat shimmers. Even the reptiles shelter underground. It is silent as the grave, burnt as desert, dry as sand ... Not a stir of wind anywhere, not a scrap of shade.

The two children sleep. They do not stir. Only the gulls move in this wilderness, and the sea. The gulls cruise and cry, leaning on the air currents, moving across and across between land and sea.

Silence. Burning heat. A child lying, a bundle left on the

station platform. A bundle kicked into a corner, kicked under a handwagon.

She is whimpering, but only half-conscious. Her tiny hands clutch at her hair and her head is bruised badly in several places. But she is too much battered to feel pain, too concussed to know where or how she is. The sun shines hard and unfriendly. In one fist she clasps the rag her mother tore from her petticoat.

The cattle-train has gone, hours before.

Someone in uniform walks along the platform. He pulls the handwagon forward. Here lies Helena, exposed like a dead animal to the open sky. She isn't conscious at all when the railway worker lifts her gently up and carries her away.

Helena's clogs got left behind. It is dusk.

'Morning, Mrs Biddell!'

'Morning, Mrs Turner!'

'Very hot today, Mrs Biddell.'

'Yes, blistering hot, Mrs Turner. And what is it today?'

'Oh the usual: a loaf of that nice granary. Terrible heat though, isn't it? Minds me of that dreadful dry summer we had. '53, wasn't it?'

'Here, this one's nice and crusty, just how you like it.'

'I remember that summer. Months and months of it we had. All through September too. I was eating my tea outside till October, that summer.'

'Anything else, Mrs Turner?'

'And do you remember those two kiddies, Mrs Biddell? The Mystery of the Missing Child? It was all the headlines that summer. Remember?'

'I do. But I don't dwell on the past, me. Take life as it comes, I do, Mrs Turner.'

'That poor little boy: dead as a doornail. And the baby

girl – his sister, remember? – disappeared into thin air. Not a trace left behind.'

'Well, what do you expect, letting two little kiddies go wandering off into the countryside. On their own. In all that heat.'

'So they reckoned it was heatstroke, did they, Mrs Biddell?'

'Oh, I didn't say that, now. Not at all. As you know, my Reggie was on that case, bless his soul. And being local he was first on the scene of the crime. As it were.'

'What I can't understand, and never could, is how they came to be up way along that wild bit of cliff there, with all those fields full of wire and goodness knows what else. You'd think they'd have been told over and over to keep away.'

'People on holidays, Mrs Turner.'

'I suppose, with some kiddies, the more you tell them not to the more they will.'

'Curiosity killed the cat, Mrs Turner.'

'That was an unsolved mystery all right. After all these years: not a sign of a murderer. And not a sign of the baby girl's body.'

'True enough, Mrs Turner. Now, was there anything else?'

'I mean, you generally get a body washed up long before the following winter. And if she fell over the cliff you'd think they'd have found the body right away, wouldn't you? What did your Reggie make of it, Mrs Biddell? I believe he was a clever one at solving a mystery.'

'Well ... being first on the scene, as it were, of course he had inside information. Reggie did say the boy had sustained injuries. But not enough to cause death. Not enough by a long chalk. But suspicion of foul play: definitely.'

'Murder, Mrs Biddell?'

'Not enough evidence, the coroner said. But my Reggie, he knew better.'

'So what about the baby girl? Was she murdered too? What happened to her? What did your Reggie make of that?'

'"Very odd," he said at the time, I remember. "Very odd," he said. "A child disappearing like that." Well, to tell the truth, he did reckon she might have been stolen.'

'Stolen, Mrs Biddell?'

'Stolen, Mrs Turner.'

'But why kill the boy – and steal the baby girl?'

'Ah, there you have it, Mrs Turner. That's the whole mystery. Doesn't add up, does it? My Reggie said that.'

'Or was it the heatstroke killed the boy?'

'My Reggie, now, bless him, told me something they kept quiet about. Very hush-hush it was.'

'Oh did he?'

'Yes he did. And it wasn't leaked out, either. Nor came up in the coroner's court. They didn't like to admit, you see, that they couldn't make head nor tail of it. So they sat on it. My Reggie told me that.'

'Oh!'

'According to my Reggie, Mrs Turner, the body gave up strange, unaccountable informations.'

'Oh!'

'Yes. And my Reggie, bless him, being first on the scene of the crime, he suspected foul play from the first. He'd swear to it, in fact. If he were alive to swear to it, of course.'

'Yes, Mrs Biddell?'

'Well. There was a strange – horrible – look about the body, according to my Reggie. "Death by poison," he said to me, that very night he came home. And that's what they found out later. My Reggie was quite right: there was poison in the blood. Riddled with it.'

'Yes? Yes?'

'And although there wasn't the slightest sign of strangulation, there was proof of death by suffocation. Suffocation by poison gas.'

'But there were injuries, as I do recall, Mrs Biddell.'

'That's true, Mrs Turner. But no serious injury. Not cause of death. No sign of struggle, either. It was in the blood: cyanide. Cyanide gas.'

'Cyanide gas?'

'Cyanide gas. Just like was used in those death camps, my Reggie said. During the war, remember? And that's why they kept it all hush hush. They couldn't make head nor tail of it.'

'Well, and we know there's no gas in these parts. We all know that, Mrs Biddell. Not a pipe up the whole coast. Not a pipe in the whole village. And yet they can have all the gas they want, up the estuary. And we don't get a look-in.'

'And that's why they kept it all a secret. Because what the powers-that-be don't understand, no one is to know about it. They thought it best forgot. But my Reggie knew all about it. He told me every detail, before he died. 'You see … there were one or two other odd things about the case.'

'Yes, Mrs Biddell?

'There was that bit of rag.'

'Rag, Mrs Biddell?'

'Yes. There was a piece of rag on the boy's hand: bound round and around his finger. He'd cut his hand somehow, it seems. So someone'd bound it up for him.'

'Someone? Well, who?'

'Linen cloth it was, nothing like anything from this part of the world. "Coarse home-made cloth. Peasant cloth." Those were my Reggie's very words. And they found a pair of shoes. The little girl's shoes. Supposedly. That was another very queer thing ...'

'Shoes, Mrs Biddell?'

'Shoes, Mrs Turner. Exactly her size. But not her own shoes. Not shoes at all, as you and I would call shoes. Clogs. Wooden clogs. Left neatly side by side at the bottom of a gate.

'As if she'd just climbed up right into heaven. Bless her little soul ...'

SONATA

•

Alex Ward

Exposition

We sit, Adam on my right, Cecilia on my left, waiting for the signal to begin. Below us the auditorium crackles with excitement. Friends and relatives, like people at a party, talking loudly, affectedly, mingle with each other exchanging pleasantries. Eyes glittering, mannerisms arch and exaggerated, they fling sequined stoles about pale shoulders, toss back unloosened glossy hair, striking poses; as if they are part of the night's performance, as, I suppose, they are. We, Adam, Cecilia and I, unable to exchange a word, a glance, waiting. This is our final performance together. Our last sonata.

Before the interval we did the solos that will determine the winner of the Rome Scholarship. I hate performing solo. It is the loneliest thing in the world. But, for the moment, we are together, a trio again. Safe. The house lights dim. We take our customary places. Our last sonata.

I love the sonata. It is so identifiably European, don't you think, so familiar in form. Like the sonnet, or a three-act play, or Marxist dialectic, with its thesis, antithesis, synthesis. And at the end, everything the same, yet everything different. A sea change, rich and strange, and very satisfying. Listen now how in the first part, the exposition, the diverse elements and themes are introduced.

See how we meld together, Adam, Cecilia and I. Weaving

the web of sound between us into something intangible, ineffable. Distinct voices but in accord. A trinity. It was always thus. We met at enrolment in our first year, and immediately struck an empathetic chord, Adam, Cecilia and I. We've been together ever since, sharing a flat, living in harmony. Never a discordant note, though we come from completely different backgrounds. Cecilia is a product of the Rudolph Steiner method of education. You know, allowing you to focus on discovering and doing 'your own thing'. Not that her 'thing' was ever in doubt. Her entire family lives for music, as she was destined to do, even before she was born. Hence her name, Cecilia, patron saint of music.

Adam is a grammar school boy. His parents are desperately, fiercely proud of him and very supportive. They wanted him to be a doctor, but when it became obvious his talents lay elsewhere, they regrouped and bought the best piano they could afford. Like Cecilia, he is quite simply brilliant.

As for me, I went to the local comprehensive, and that about sums me up. Oh yes, I have hard-won technique, as our director says, but lack inspiration, passion. A-1 for effort. That's me. As for my mum, she thinks this 'music thing' unnatural. I can't talk to her about it. She gets this buttoned-up look. She'd rather I worked in the mini-mart. In her view, you leave home only when you get married. Boys, babies, booze and bingo are the extent of her expectations. We have little in common. I don't go back much. The flat's my home now.

Development
Music is moving along the strings, up the bow, into my fingers. From my fingers down the bow, into the strings. Round and round the sound goes — no beginning, no end.

And we, too, are enclosed in this circuit of sound, Adam, Cecilia and I, oblivious to the dark, expectant hush below. My heart thrills as the familiar themes from the first part are reintroduced, extended, and new themes juxtaposed. A fluent conversation, developing slowly at first then growing increasingly urgent, frenetic, as one, then the other, running counterpoint to the melodic line, strives for self-expression, daringly endangering the unity.

I am frightened of discord, frightened of change. After tonight, everything will change. It is already changing. I hear it in the music, frightening and wonderful. Adam and I were talking earlier, before our solos. 'Cecilia must win, you know,' he said. 'It's expected of her. I won't put up a fight.' I argued with him, reminded him of his parents' expectations. 'It's not the same for me,' he said. 'I've already fulfilled their wildest dreams, and most of my own.' But nothing I said broke his resolve. 'Don't look so worried,' he said. 'I shall play *well*. I won't let you down.'

Oh Adam, I won't let you down either. I knew he'd be mad if he found out but I went in search of Cecilia, appealed to her. Her eyes widened momentarily, but she kept her cool. 'How very sweet, how very unprofessional,' she said, all but smiling. 'What will you say to him?' I pressed. 'Nothing,' she said. 'I'm not supposed to know, am I?' Her pale mediaeval face flushed lightly and she made much of fiddling with the tight bun she always wore, but that was it. The subject was closed. Seeing my surprise, confusion, she put out her hand and touched me gently on the arm. 'Look, I must get ready. But don't worry. I won't let you down,' she said, and was gone. The same grace note struck again, but empty of meaning. I ran to look for Adam, but was too late. The solos had begun.

Snared in the spotlight, Adam takes his seat at the piano.

For me, this is always the worst moment of a performance. Silence breathes up out of the darkness like the susperation of the earth at night. Enthralling, thrilling, terrifying, unbearable. But Adam is at ease, at home, as he settles himself, pauses, begins to play. And I am free to dwell on him, oh so familiar, yet presently so remote. His dark hair is pulled back into a thick ponytail. It has the texture and vibrancy of horsehair. I know, I have trimmed it often enough, letting it run through my fingers, playing with it, not wanting to let go. He arches over the keyboard, his face hidden from me. The music leaps and rattles and crashes in thundering chords, making a white water of sound in which we drown. Then it broadens into calmer, lyrical cadences, proceeding with a tender energy that is deeply expressive, wholly enchanting. Rapture. Then silence. He turns to the audience, smiles. The applause, immediate and unequivocal, engulfs him.

As we pass in the wings, he whispers 'Go to it, lass.' My moment of torture has arrived. I step out into the light and bow my head like a lamb held for the sacrificial blow. I am paralysed with terror. Literally petrified. Then technique takes over, and I can breathe, move, think again. Adam and Cecilia. He said she must win. But surely he cannot lose now, not after that. I do not want him to lose. I do not want him to win, to go away. Confused, my thoughts come tumbling as the notes spill from my bow, discordant thoughts, notes. And out of the confusion, the sudden sharp sweet pain of recognition at something long hidden, a sealed chamber abruptly exposed to searing light. The simple equation – three, take away one, leaves two. Someone has been chosen, albeit informally. The implications course through me. Adam and I, the two of us, in *our* flat. Electric excitement thrills in shock waves through all the fibres of my being. Adam, oh Adam. I am Alice falling down the rabbit-hole, rushing to some unknown, inescapable destiny. It was always thus, but I could not see it. Defining, as I have, everything in terms of the trio, held in suspension. Three, take away one, leaves two. Ah Adam, I *am* the music, reborn, reformed, renewed.

Adam is waiting in the wings as Cecilia passes. I cannot stop shaking and he wraps me in some cape he's found, and holds me tight, calming me. Cecilia and her cello glow under the single spot, transfigured. Gone the secure knot of ginger hair. Unleashed, it tumbles in an abundant marmalade cascade of copper lights and depths about her delicate white shoulders. Her gooseberry-green eyes are dark and sparkling as she briefly turns in our direction, her lips as if stained with some strange juice. A goddess in truth. The music drips mellifluous as honey, a perfect confection, sweet, so sweet. I am happy with her, sorry for her. I long to tell her my discovery, know I shall not, knowing there will be no more shared confidences in the kitchen. No more unsuitable suitors tactfully dislodged by her for me, me for her. The bridge between us has been irretrievably broken down. Regret and anticipation war within me. Applause. She is coming towards us. Adam relinquishes me. How cold it feels without him. And so, as I have said before, and so to our last sonata.

Recapitulation

I am frightened of change, but change is the creative essence of the sonata. The form contains and restrains us, Adam, Cecilia and me. Held in an aesthetic stasis, yet moving imperceptibly towards a resolution. We return to our original themes. In our beginning is our end. I hear them talking to each other, the piano, the cello, and my violin breaks in on them pleading, begging, weeping to be heard. They are singing to each other now, neither closing in nor moving apart. My violin voice fading down the air, plaintive, distant. And then we come together again, the key note like a tether from which we have strayed but to which we must return, drawing us in. And abruptly it is over, our last sonata. The spell is broken.

Out of the darkness applause bursts like some enormous exotic flower matured in secret. We take our bows and await our fate. The announcement of the scholarship winner is imminent. Suddenly, I am propelled forward. Alone. Dazzled, I hear the words 'Perfect technique infused with deep passion. An inspired performance.' Spontaneous bravos erupt from he auditorium. Flowers shower down at my feet. In disbelief, I turn round to look at Adam and Cecilia. They are standing close together, holding hands, smiling at me for all the world like proud parents. The sense of loss is shattering.

Coda

In a sudden flash of insight, my future is revealed to me. The world is all before me, its vast stages raked to my advantage. I shall return, but only occasionally, perhaps to stay with my dear friends Adam and Cecilia in some house of theirs filled with music, with children. Adam and Cecilia, teachers of music – very unprofessional, very sweet.

MARY KATE

•

Jenny Sullivan

Why do I dust?

More takes to the air to settle back than ever sticks to the duster. Housework, running a home, it's like having someone always nag-nagging at you. Only this isn't a home, not really. It's just a house with two people in it, and a ghost or two.

Wasn't always like this. When I was little and Mammy and Patrick were here, we'd gather round Mammy at the piano on Sunday evenings and Michael would sing flat and make us laugh. Dada was kinder to me then. Oh, I knew even when I was little that he didn't love me. But I understood, I was only a girl.

Then Patrick was killed and Michael went away and Da changed. He'd always been one to lash out if we got in his way when he'd had a drink, but it got worse after Patrick, the shouting and the blows. One night, even though my head was stuffed hard under all my pillows I heard a crash that made me run downstairs, certain that the roof had fallen in at the very least. He'd hit out at the piano, and the lid hung crooked, a great crack striking across it.

Dada pushed past me and stumped upstairs. Mammy didn't look at me, but she lifted up the broken lid and fitted it back so it stayed, and straightened the picture which had hung over it ever since I could remember. Mammy dusted that picture every day, tenderly buffing the dust off the frame, huffing on the glass and wiping the film away, looking the way she did when she washed my face before Mass, with her head cocked on one side to see me better, checking there was no jam at the corners of my mouth.

The face in the picture was young, although the picture was old: the sepia print was beginning to fade.

I never knew his name, the priest in the picture, only that he'd gone to Our Lady's Convent with Dada and Mammy when they were all wee. Mammy sometimes put a small vase of flowers on a little lace doily at the end of the piano to hide the crack. She'd take the wee vase, with a few Michaelmas daisies from the yard in it, and she'd put it right square under the picture the way she put flowers before the statue of the Blessed Virgin in their bedroom. Then she'd take her hand away, just for a few seconds, and smile a little smile. Then her hand would steal back to the vase, and she'd s-l-i-d-e it slowly on its mat all the way to the far end of the piano.

The first time Da hit her in the daytime, that's what she'd done. She'd put the wee vase down under the photo, and right then rackety Mrs Thomas knocked the door to beg the loan of a few potatoes, and Mammy went into the scullery to fetch. I was reading, balled in a chair lulled by Sunday smells and sounds and the afterglow of Mass when Da came in. He froze dead still in the doorway, looking from the flowers to the picture and back again, then stood in front of them, his back to me. Mammy came in, and stopped, and I saw his thick neck contract, and the muscles of his shoulders tighten. The great blow he pitched at Mammy knocked her almost through the wall, and the backswing took the vase down and pushed the picture crooked.

Then he strode out to the street, his face black, in just his shirt-sleeves, and on the Sabbath! Mammy crouched down over the tangle of flowers and glass, not crying despite the blow she'd taken, but slowly picking up the shards and placing them in the pouch of her apron while her eye swelled up like a purple plum.

There was something odd about Da and that picture: when visitors came he'd always call their eyes to it, he'd draw Mammy close into his side with his arm about her shoulders and he'd say 'You remember him? Such a sweet, saintly man. From Our Lady's Convent he went straight as God's best arrow to the seminary. He's in Canada, now, is he not, Katie?' And Mammy would smile and nod, but she'd not look up, and her fingers would be twist, twisting in her apron pockets.

He beat her often when Patrick was taken, and after Michael's job took him away and it was just Mammy and him and me, and there was no one to see or stop him.

Then Mammy died, and after the neighbours had gone, and the funeral meats had been finished, he tried to turn me into Mammy. I did my best to keep the house nice like Mammy had it, but what with working at the store it was sometimes too late to buy something nice for his dinner, and then didn't he give me the rough tongue!

One night, not long after Mammy died, I heard him come in, noisy with the drink, and stumble up the stairs. But he stopped outside my door, and I could hear the sound of his breathing, in, out, in: slow and heavy. He stood so long, ages it seemed, that I slid silently from my bed and softly turned the key in the lock. I didn't even know what had made me do it until I saw the handle slowly turn.

He never hit me, though, not until Owen. Ah, God, wasn't he the handsomest thing I'd ever set eyes on? Welsh, he was of course, and born in one of the mining towns up beyond Cardiff, but his Mammy and Da had died and he was lodging a bit up the road from our house between his trips to sea. When he took up with me I thought I'd died and gone to heaven with his uniform and his handsome face with the wee lines white in the tan around his eyes. He spent free, took me to expensive places to eat and drink, and walked me home from work with my arm tucked, so, through his. I kept it from Da easy because of his shifts.

But one evening there was nothing to unload at the docks, and he pitched up early in an evil mood because of the week's short wage, and he caught us on the doorstep. Not that we were doing anything bad; we were just talking, our faces close and the street door a little open for me to go in soon and start his tea, when he came.

He grabbed at the soft part of my arm just above my elbow, and thrust me before him into the house. It was weeks before his finger-marks faded. He shouted Owen away, and slammed the door in his face. Then he punched me half senseless. I wanted Owen to break down the door and come flying in for me like an avenging angel. But maybe he couldn't hear the sound of the blow and the shouts through the door.

So I had to be brave for myself and stand up to Da and tell him he had no right to treat me so. 'I am not your wife to beat,' I said, so afraid that my heart thumped like a great drum and my legs would barely hold me.

'You're not my daughter, either,' he said, shoving me into the parlour and pointing to the innocent, joyful face above the clerical collar, the sepia receding into the dusk of the summer's evening.

'There's your father, him, William, my best friend and the best man who ever lived. Your Mammy tempted him, and in his sweet innocence he fell. Oh, there's no doubt who your Mammy is, with you panting after a sailor like a tuppenny slut.'

I snatched at my thoughts, feeling my world shift and suddenly begin to move in a new orbit. 'If he's my father,' I flung back, 'then I owe you nothing more. I'm free of you. I'll go to Canada to him instead. He will be a good man if Mammy loved him: he'd not beat me.'

He sneered, the gathering dusk darkening the hair on his fleshy wrists until he looked almost black. 'You'll not find him in Canada. When the Bishop heard what she'd done to him he sent him back to the seminary to be purified of her mortal wickedness, but that poor, good man couldn't face the shame of the guilt she'd left him with. He hanged himself the day he got there.'

My mother's face as he hugged her before the picture was as clear in my mind as the sly malice that had been on his own. Twenty years she'd suffered for her small sin, and she died without his pity.

I went on living there, and I went on seeing Owen who made a show of righteous anger when he saw my bruised face. He offered to batter the daylights out of Da for what he'd done, but the threat didn't go deep.

But after, I found I was looking carefully at Owen. The way his eyes followed the jaunty girls in the streets, his traveller's tales that changed with each telling, and the size of the big fine house he owns, so he says, in Patagonia, grew and shrank: a fisherman's tale. He's free with his money except he sometimes has nothing less than a £5 note and has to borrow smaller from the bit of pay I manage to keep back for myself from the housekeeping.

I'd almost decided to go with him to Patagonia, but – but I think that if I do I'll only change one man like Da for another. I'll tell him, I won't let him wait, not knowing. If he does feel for me, I'd not want to hurt him. But then I'm away.

I wasn't there for Patrick, but a nurse wrote a kind letter to Mammy telling that he'd not suffered, his death had been quick, and he had died happy in his faith. But perhaps I could be there for some other girl's brother, to help his passing. I'd be a good nurse, I'm gentle and not afraid of the sight of blood, and they are calling for nurses at the front.

I've left himself a note, and another for Michael. I've packed my few things and taken enough money from the jar on the mantel to pay my fare to London.

Before I closed my suitcase, I took the picture from the wall and wrapped it in the lace runner from the sideboard, putting it face down on top of my clothes so the glass won't break.

For who will take care of a man if his own daughter does not?

HESTER AND LOUISE

·

Siân James

When I was a girl women looked their age, particularly if they were widows. My grandmother could only have been in her early sixties when I remember her, but she had settled comfortably into old age; wiry grey hair scraped back into a tight bun, round cheeks reddened by sun and broken veins, dark shapeless clothes, grey woollen stockings baggy round the ankles.

She'd once been a district nurse. On the mantlepiece in the parlour there was a photograph of her standing importantly at someone's front door, large bag in hand, round hat pulled down to the eyebrows; but I found it difficult to believe in this starched image, could only see the untidy old woman she'd become, shooing the hens away from the back door with a dirty tea cloth, bending to cut a lettuce in the garden, her large bottom in the air, standing at the gate, squinting into the sun, her heavy breasts supported on her folded arms.

I stayed with her for five or six weeks every summer, not for her benefit or for mine, but because it eased the pressure on my parents who kept a dairy in St John's Wood.

I liked London far better than the Welsh countryside. I missed the Friday night dancing class, the Saturday morning cinema, the big public library which was only two streets away, and my friends, Jennifer and Mandy.

There was no dancing class, cinema or library in Bryn-awel and the village children scorned me. The much-praised fresh air always seemed to have an overlay of cows' shit; I much preferred stale air with petrol fumes.

I didn't like Gran's meals either: runny boiled eggs with orange yolks for breakfast, dirty-looking potatoes, greens and grey meat for dinner, brown bread with cheese and salad for supper, with the occasional addition of a cater-pillar or little black flies.

I didn't like my bedroom, though it had once been my father's; the bed was hard, the pillows lumpy and the sheets rough. But worst of all, my grandmother had no bathroom and expected me to strip-wash in the back kitchen with carbolic soap and the same wet towel that she'd used. The summer when I was twelve, she promised to keep out when I was washing, but twice she forgot and came barging in, and once the coalman came to the back door and saw me in vest and knickers. 'Oh, the man will never be the same again,' was all she said when I complained.

When I was thirteen, I begged my parents to let me stay home; I pleaded and cried, promising to serve in the shop, wash dishes, anything. 'I'll do anything, anything, but please don't send me away to Gran's.'

My father thought I was daft. He and his brother Bob had had an idyllic childhood, he said; all the freedom of the fields and woods, fishing, ratting, scrumping apples, help-ing the farmers with the harvest, earning sixpence a day. 'This one's a girl, though, Isaac,' my mother said, 'she likes different sorts of things, girl things, going round Wool-worth's and Boots, buying shampoo, trying on lipsticks, things like that. Try to understand.'

'It's not just those things,' I said, since he was looking at me as though he'd never seen me before. 'It's just that Gran doesn't have a bathroom and I don't have any privacy. And I'm not a child any more. I have my periods now and I wear a bra. And I'm not going to bath in the back kitchen and you shouldn't expect me to.'

That shut him up. He could never tolerate any talk of bodily functions. And my mother promised to write a very polite letter to Gran, explaining how I felt.

We had a letter back by return of post.

She quite understood the position. I was going through a little phase, that was all, and they were not to worry. She'd spoken to Hester and Louise, the Arwel sisters, though, and I was most welcome to use their bathroom any time I wanted to, twice a day if I'd a mind. And they, as I probably remembered, had an all-pink bathroom the size of a small ballroom with bottles of this and that and loofahs and sponges and a special brush for scrubbing your back, pale grey carpet on the floor and a little fluffy cover on the WC.

'The Arwel sisters,' my father said, casting his eyes to the ceiling.

'I'll go,' I said. 'I love Miss Hester and Miss Louise. The Sundays they invite me to their house after church are the only days I enjoy.'

'She's a girl, Isaac,' my mother said again. 'Try to understand.'

Miss Hester and Miss Louise didn't seem to belong in Brynawel, but to a world I knew only from the cinema. I'd often try to describe them to my friends, Jennifer and Mandy. 'No, they're not really young, perhaps thirty-five or so, even forty, and they're like ladies in old-fashioned films with tiny waists and delicate faces like flowers. Well, I think they may have had sweethearts once, but perhaps

they were killed in the war. No, they're definitely not spinsters, spinsters are altogether different. No, they don't have
jobs, they just have money, plenty of money, so they can do
whatever they want to. Sometimes they hire a car to take
them out shopping or to the seaside or to church on Sunday. Otherwise they stay at home doing tapestry, reading
magazines and changing their clothes. Oh, they're very
gentle and kind. Just think of me going there each day!
And I know they'll give me home-made lemonade and iced
biscuits every time. I'm really looking forward to staying
with Gran this year.'

The sisters called on the very afternoon I arrived to remind
me of their promise. 'Isn't she pretty,' one said, smoothing
down my rough curly hair. 'Isn't she pretty,' the other re-
plied. They always repeated each other's pronouncements.
'Hasn't she grown tall and slender.' 'Hasn't she grown tall
and slender.'

'Don't turn her head,' Gran said. 'She's foolish enough
already.'

'We've heard different. We've heard that she had an
excellent end of term report and that she's a marvellous
little pianist.'

'A marvellous little pianist, as well.'

'We want her to play for us. We've had our piano tuned.'

'We've had our old piano tuned specially.'

I'd forgotten the way they so often stood with their arms
clasped tightly round each other's waists, as though they
wanted to be one person instead of two.

They were dressed that day in cream high-necked blouses,
full dark green skirts, black belts pulled tight and cream
high-heeled shoes. They always dressed identically, though
they weren't twins. Hester was a year and a half older and

she was also a little taller and perhaps a little more elegant. Louise's eyes were a brighter blue, though, and her lips were fuller. I could never decide which was the more beautiful.

'Well, I must ask you to go now,' Gran said, 'because I always listen to my serial at four o'clock. I'll send the girl round after supper.'

I could never understand how Gran had the nerve to treat them so casually, even rudely, when she was so ugly and poor and they were so beautiful and so rich.

'Who told them about my report?' I asked her when they'd left.

'I did, of course. I told them you were going to college to be a teacher. In case they have any ideas of turning you into a ladies' maid.'

'Are they so rich?'

'Gracious me, yes. Their father had the best farm in the county, but when he knew he was dying and with no son and heir, he had to sell it all, land and livestock, to buy an annuity for those two. Their mother had died, you see, when they were toddlers, soon after Louise was born, and he spoiled them, of course, and everybody spoiled them. Even when they were schoolgirls, they never had to do a hand's turn for themselves, let alone anything in the house or the farm. It was hard on him in the end. But what could he expect? He'd brought them up to be butterflies.'

'Why didn't they get married?'

'No one from around here was stupid enough to ask them, I suppose. To tell you the truth, your uncle Bob seemed to be thick with them at one time, but he never seemed to know which one of them he liked best and then he was called up and met your auntie Dilys, so he lost them both. He was a born farmer, Bob was, ready to do a day and a half's work every day. Their father would have been proud to have him as a son-in-law, and he would have been the making of those girls, but which one of them?'

'But which one of them?'

'God help us, if you're going to start being an echo like those two.'

'God help us,' I began. But she cuffed me on the head and turned the wireless on.

To think that one of them could have been my auntie. My auntie Dilys was nice enough, but she wasn't special in any way.

If I hurried over my supper and the washing up, I had two whole hours to spend at Arwel and I savoured every moment.

I'd be shown first into the drawing room where we'd have coffee, real coffee, served in a silver coffee pot, where I sat in a fat, velvet chair and was passed a cup and saucer of green and gold eggshell china, pink crystals of sugar and exotic dark chocolates. After this delightful ritual, I might look at their photograph albums: two plump little girls sitting together on a garden seat, chubby legs and solemn round faces, two ten-year-olds in frilly party dresses with ribbons in their hair, two young ladies in their first ball gowns.

'This one is you, isn't it Hester?' I'd ask.

'Wait a minute, now. I really can't tell. No one seemed sure, even at the time. They always called us the girls or the sisters, you know, never our names. We hardly knew ourselves which of us was which, did we Louise?'

'We hardly knew ourselves, did we, Hester?'

The house was so beautiful, so wickedly luxurious; thick carpets everywhere and floor-length velvet curtains, heavy as the falling darkness outside. They lent me a dressing gown of plum-coloured chenille, and after I'd bathed and washed my hair, they'd take me to their bedroom and take it in turn to brush my hair, brushing gently, gently, almost as though they were in a trance. They each had an ivory hairbrush, I remember, one with a silver H on its back and the other an L. I wished my hair was long and straight and raven-black instead of short and reddish-brown. Gran had forbidden me to use make-up, but they insisted that complexion milk didn't count, so they smoothed it into my face and my neck and my shoulders. It felt soft and silky and smelt of little white roses, so different from Gran's carbolic soap. 'She's got such delicate skin, hasn't she Hester?' 'Her skin is as soft as a baby's, isn't it, Louise?' Afterwards I was encouraged to try on their perfumes – luckily Gran had lost her sense of smell – and I loved repeating their grand French names; *Je Reviens, Bal de Nuit, Ma Griffe, L'air du Temps, Mon Désir, Arpège.*

Their house had several bedrooms, six or seven I should think, but they slept together in the largest and grandest one in the front. (The long small room at the back of the house was where their maid, housekeeper, cook slept, a bustling little woman called Gladys who had been with them since their birth. They always got her to walk home with me, but she never came very far because she was frightened of the dark and I wasn't.)

They slept in a high, old-fashioned bed with a brass bedstead. The quilt was a bright turquoise silk, the colour matching the tiny rosebuds on the cream wallpaper, and the carpets, the heavy curtains and the satin lampshades were a deep voluptuous pink. There was a highly-polished bedside table on either side of the wide bed with a framed photograph on each.

One evening Hester picked up the photograph from her side, gazing at it as though willing me to notice it. I didn't need much prompting. 'What a handsome man,' I said. He was handsome; dark curly hair, slanting eyes, straight nose and full, curved lips. And as I might have guessed, Louise then brought me the photograph from her bedside, and at first I thought it was the same man in a different pose.

'Brothers,' I said then. 'Twin brothers.'

They smiled at each other, but didn't volunteer any information and I was too shy to ask.

One evening towards the end of my holiday, though, when it was mothy and dark as Gladys walked me back to Gran's, I ventured to ask her about the handsome young men.

She seemed flustered. 'What young men?' 'The brothers in the photographs on the bedside tables.' 'Yes. Very nice young gentlemen,' she said then. 'Sons of a very good family. Not from round here at all.'

'What happened to them?'

'Killed. Killed in the war.'

'Both of them?'

'Both of them. Nice young men. Real gentlemen. Not from these parts, of course.'

'Poor Miss Hester and Miss Louise.'

'Yes indeed. 1944. Ten years ago now, very near. And never anyone else after.'

'Gran told me that my uncle Bob was friendly with them once.'

She was furious. 'Nonsense. Your Uncle Bob was a labourer. He worked on the farm but he never came to the house. He knew his place, Bob did. Your Gran likes to boast, that's all. I'm turning back now. You can run from here, can't you.'

'Gladys was in a stew when I told her about uncle Bob courting the sisters,' I told Gran.

'She knows nothing about it. She was in Swansea nursing her mother during the war. It was I who had to look after them then.'

'Do you mean when their young men were killed?'

'Their young men? What young men are you talking about now?'

'Real gentlemen, Gladys said they were. Sons of a very good family.'

'Gladys is getting soft in the head.'

Now that I had my interesting association with the Arwel sisters to sustain me, Gran didn't seem so much of a trial; she often seemed nothing but a fairly harmless relic from an unhygienic past. Sometimes in the evening, I sat at her side on the old rexine sofa, leaning my head on her shoulder, almost able to ignore the dirty-dishcloth smell coming from her.

'Tell me a secret, Gran.'

'What about?'

'You know. About the sisters. About their past. Tell me why they're different from other people.'

'I'll tell you when you're older.'

'Gran, you'll be dead when I'm older.'

She chuckled at that. She liked straight talk. She leaned forward, looked me straight in the eye and cleared her throat. 'They never had any men friends, real gentlemen or otherwise. They only had one man between them and he … he was an Italian prisoner of war.'

'Is that all?'

'Isn't that enough?'

'He was a handsome man, anyway. I saw his photo, two of his photos.'

'Married, of course.'

'So they were in disgrace, is that it?'

'You could say that, yes.'

I could see her hesitating about going on, but I squeezed her arm and gave her an imploring look. 'Their father found him in bed with them, you see. In between them, he said. That seemed to be the last straw. I don't think he'd have minded quite so much if he'd been either firmly on one side or the other, but there he was cuddled up between them. All three of them naked as babies, he said.'

'Naked?' I swallowed hard. I knew about sexual inter-course, yes, but I found certain of the details very unsavoury.

'Naked as new-born babies.'

'And after the war, I suppose he went back to Italy?' I tried to keep the quiver out of my voice.

'Gran paused again. 'No. No, sometime later he was found shot in Henblas woods.'

'Murdered? Do you mean murdered?'

'That's right. Murdered. The Italians weren't exactly loved at that time, especially the very handsome ones. No one found out who'd shot him. There were no clues. It could have been anybody, I suppose.'

'Poor things. Poor Hester. Poor Louise.'

'Don't cry. You wanted the truth and now you must accept it.'

'And you had to look after them. Were they very un-happy?'

'They were, of course. Very unhappy.'

She glanced at me again, as though wondering how much more I could take. 'Go on,' I said.

'And pregnant as well. Very pregnant. Five or six months pregnant.'

'Both of them?'

'Both of them. Well, that's what happens when you lie naked in bed with a handsome man, especially an Italian.'

'Both of them pregnant?'

'Yes.'

'Oh Gran, whatever happened to their little babies?'

'I looked after their babies, one boy, one girl, until they were old enough to be adopted. And it was straight after that that their father died.'

'Gran, it's a terrible story, a cruel story.'

'That's why I didn't want you to hear it.'

We were both silent for a while. I felt there was a hand twisting my stomach. I wanted to be sick, wanted to vomit up everything I'd heard.

'But they've still got each other, haven't they,' I said at last.

'Yes, they've still got each other, God help them, foolish as they are.'

I thought of them, their arms clasped tightly round each other's waists, repeating each other's sentences, spending hours laying out their dresses on the wide bed deciding which to wear, trying on their lovely jewellery.

'Shall I spend the whole day with them tomorrow, Gran? Because it's my last day? They said I could.'

'Then I suppose you can. Silly girl. Go to bed now. You can come again next year ... unless I'm dead before that, of course.'

'Oh Granma, don't die,' I said crossly.